First Paperback Edition 2010
Published in Canada
Book design: D.Grîn

ISBN: 978-0-9810117-1-4

Voices

(Kyle Muntz)

*the page
before*

Voices

II

If walls

could speak, then maybe
the world would

still be full
of conversation.

I remember

once, back in a place that wasn't quite like this, I thought maybe I wasn't doing everything right. I've always been like that, saying strange things to myself. My friends say I'm not the same anymore, but that's not true. They just don't know what it means to hear at an angle.

If a clown tosses a ball into the air, sometime soon it has to fall. The world is a theater of gravitation. In school they teach us to believe what we hear. Then

they tell us to speak clearly.

::::::::::::::::::::

I found Jacob hiding in that place he always hung out. He had dirt on his hands and more dirt on his hair. His shoulders shook, and he pressed deeper into the corner, back here where it smelled like shit, where the spiders were. He told me to be quiet and get down, it isn't safe. I got down.

"What's going on?"

He shook. Getting down. I didn't care to know. From the distance came pounding feet, wind and breath, sweat, dust, eyes and hands. He shook, fearing. I asked if he was okay, but he didn't know how to answer. A cardboard box rolled over: stained, covered in creases. It made a sound and he jumped, hugging the dumpster.

"How many are there?"

He made fingers. Five. Wouldn't tell me what he'd done, but I already knew. I asked if he could stand. He couldn't, but I forced him. I handed him a pipe. The pipe didn't look quite right when he held it (shaking, knobby, he wasn't breathing well), but that was fine too.

Voices

"Okay," I said, "here's what we're going to do."
But I didn't need to tell him. He already knew.
They came quick around the corner.
We did it.
We ran.

::::::::::::::::::::

We jumped over a gray wall. There was tall grass on the other side. Tall grass doesn't belong in the city. It grew in ugly clumps, moldy green, patching up, five fingers of nature, budding through. I told him to quit making sounds. He obviously couldn't.

Earlier that week I'd seen Jacob getting thrown out. He was always too liberal with his hands. They don't like liberals in the city. In the city you keep your own space, you prioritize, you draw lines to keep the world away. Jacob didn't understand that, but neither did I. It isn't about understanding here. I understood that already.

::::::::::::::::::::

We came out somewhere by neither of our houses. We'd never been here before. This place didn't have any right to exist: a suburban sprawl, houses and tender lines, old men, old lives. We beat three mailboxes before we left.

That's not true.

We talked about it, but I wrote a poem instead, in bright colors. The next day I saw my poem on the news. Some guy kept saying kids were so bad these days, those horrible kids. I smiled. He was old, he was fat, and his house was a temple of language. I wonder if he understood what I wrote. I'm sure he didn't.

::::::::::::::::::::

When a beam of light shines, it catches the dust and makes it alive. No, the dust was always there, it just needs the light make it glow.

::::::::::::::::::::

We found Travis playing basketball. He wasn't doing well, but he never did well, and that had never bothered him before. Bouncing, he made the court his own. Or he thought he did. That was enough for him; it would always be enough for him. One day, he said, he'd be the best in the world. He wouldn't, but I think he already knew. We played for a while. Jacob was better. I was better too. We planted roots at Travis's house. Jacob did liberal things with Travis's sister. They hadn't thought to tell him.

  I stayed for half an hour. Travis wanted to have a conversation about politics. None of us knew what we were talking about, but that was part of the idea. Jacob left a few minutes in to take a piss. He'd been gone fifteen minutes. I was sure he'd be gone fifteen more. Travis had basketball posters on his walls, and he never stopped wanting to fly. His room bled bright color. I set my camera on the bed.

    Ten lights

  on
  to crush dreams

    that aren't quite   dreams.

  If I were playing games with words, I would say Travis wanted to play poker. I didn't have the money. Jacob was in the next room with Travis's sister, poking her. Travis still didn't know. Sometimes I'm not a very good friend. I thought of telling him. I didn't.

::::::::::::::::::::

Travis and I have poignant conversations sometimes. This was not one of them. As teenagers, we aren't any good at being poignant. It clashes with our oldest, most profound traditions.

::::::::::::::::::::

That night I went to lie alone looking at the sky, on a hill outside the city. Geysers of light shot up, subtle, a dim electricity. On a corner a couple walked by holding hands. They were probably in love, if you put faith in vision. There was a prostitute on this street I'd always wanted to meet. People paid her to be an object. I wonder if it kept her from being real.

Voices

When I was young I'd come here sometimes to paint pictures. They were never any good. Now sometimes I come here to write poems. I got a shot of the sky, made a sweep of the skyline. A bistro closed for the night. There was a place I wanted to be. I got there too late.

I guess I fell asleep. Perception became a wave of falling, then I was watching streams of pure light, shower of stars, white as transcendence, still falling. I'd been having this dream for years. Whenever I woke I'd try to write about it, but I never did a good job.

I've been hearing voices.

I met her again, and meeting her was
        beautiful. She made the world
beautiful. I ran my hands through her hair, and it felt
beautiful. When she laughed, it was
                    beautiful. She walked and it was
      beautiful. She made me think
beautiful thoughts, and when she spoke, it was
beautiful too.

::::::::::::::::::::

... no, I've been exaggerating.
I do that a lot.

::::::::::::::::::::

We sat and talked for a while on the veranda. Before that night I had no idea: *the immensity of what* it meant to be a veranda. I remember. It was just a place, boarded, where the flatness was. But she changed it into an element of herself, with chairs.

She asked my name again. But it wasn't part of me anymore.

"But that's ridiculous," she said, of course I knew. Her skin shone in the light. She leaned against me, obtusely real, not quite playing in her element.

"It's not fair," she said. "I already told you my name."

"I'll forget yours if you promise to forget mine."

"Why?"

"It's a secret."

Voices

We kissed for a while. I whispered my name in her ear. I'm not any good at keeping secrets. She had her hand around my back, her leg against my thigh. We kissed some more. I wrote a poem for her. We tried to count prime numbers. The grasshoppers watched. A star fell out of the sky.

::::::::::::::::::::

I mentioned her to my friend the next day. He didn't understand who she was. I could only tell him she was beautiful. He said that didn't do any good, you can't describe a person like that. I said I know, people are body and soul and compound, but it would have to do.

::::::::::::::::::::

I am a hypocrite and a liar.
    Somebody broke off a piece of glass
    in my heart.

::::::::::::::::::::

I visited Jacob in his corner again. He was smoking. I turned a cigarette down and kicked over the cardboard box.
    "Why do you come back here?"
    He shrugged. "Why not?"
    "Are they chasing you again?"
    "Not yet. Or I don't think so."
    I walked around for a minute. My back hurt. Jacob sat next to a big nest of spiders. They hadn't gotten him yet. He had dirt on his face again for no reason this time, and he let up a trail of smoke, widening, one twisting, turning strand, rising and rising. No matter where life took him, he would never visit the stratosphere. I wondered if he would miss it. Together.
    "I never should've helped you, you know."
    "Yeah," he said. "I know."

::::::::::::::::::::

A star fell out of the sky. No, the star was still falling. It fell, and wound, and came back to earth, strands of the psyche, a firey, flaming dusk. I held her tighter, and we talked for a while on the veranda. Our fingers were of mesh of touch and sharing. I kissed the nape of her neck.

I'd seen her the day before, remembering the first time we met. Our eyes caught, and she made me want to stare. Chance meetings desist from me. We ran from each other, making circles, playing dangerous games in the roses.

She tasted like moonlight and nocturnal beauty. No, that's not true either. She tasted like vodka and lips, tongue and teeth. Neither of us understood beauty, though I think we wanted to. Life would be so much simpler if we could pretend not to have names.

::::::::::::::::::::::

I went to visit the guy whose house I'd painted. He didn't recognize me because there was nothing to remember. His house looked the same; his street looked the same; his world was unchanging and the same. Mailboxes, lampposts, sidewalks and toy slides, I'd been here before now, so it was different, but it felt strange to come back. I didn't belong here. Our frequencies clashed all wrong. I still wanted to break a mailbox.

I knocked on the door. He answered fat and bald, ripples, the titanic bulge, his hairy, hairy chest, warbling chins, swinging gut. His house smelled like a department store. It was much cleaner than he was.

He asked who I was. Impatiently. I knew he'd be impatient.

I said I was here doing an interview; a documentary; whatever you wanted to call it. There were these kids around here, I said, these really bad kids, and they were getting to be such a problem. He agreed. His chest puffed. Importantly. I knew he'd think he was important.

"It all goes wrong," he said, "when the kids stop saying "sir". It all goes wrong. There's no respect in the world today. There's no consequence," choking, "and the world's going to hell. I have proof." His chins jiggled, multiplied, jiggled again. He said: "The world's going to hell, I say. When the respect goes."

He certainly talked like he was important.

And like most important people, he had very little to say.

::::::::::::::::::::::

Voices

"I went to that guy's house earlier today," I said. "I got it all on tape."

Jacob looked up. He'd gotten pretty drunk. His eyes wandered, and his face sagged. Jacob's face did that, wilting, one eye down, like the proverbial neighbor's dog, flee-bitten, infected. He existed to be spat on, a worthless little boy in a cold place, wearing passed down clothes and worthless skin. There was no place for him here, no corner to set him down.

He said I always got things on tape, so why should he care. His head wobbled, bobbing. He didn't understand self-awareness. I walked around a bit more. The spiders might bite him. I wondered why I should care.

::::::::::::::::::::

I saw her again that day. I saw her. She looked beautiful, her eyes looked beautiful, her arms looked beautiful. We passed and she went the other way. The crowd drew a boundary between us. We pretended not to see.

::::::::::::::::::::

It was my friend's party. I didn't want to go. I was busy tonight, I said. My friend said I wrote enough, and no one understood my poetry, so what did it matter? There would be girls there. He'd probably be getting laid. I said good luck. But that night I didn't write any poetry. I went.

I'd gotten there late. There were kids in the yard, screaming. Someone had tried to flatten the mailbox. I wished I'd gotten it first. Inside the lights were on, and the music was on, and the door was open. I wondered how many people I knew. Most of them. A kid with green spikes vomited in the yard, spraying strangely scented stomach, peculiarly thin.

"You okay dude?"

"Yeah..." he said. "Yeah, I'll be okay."

He heaved. His shoulders shook. He looked to be in agonizing pain, showing it. His face crinkled; his hair shook. He tried to hug me (with a tackling motion), but he smelled like puke, so I backed away in time. He had a cool tattoo.

::::::::::::::::::::

"The kids don't have any respect," he said. I penciled in the rest.

He was obviously used to being a speaker, and having people listen. It was repulsive, his inclination to the stage. I wondered if he deserved my respect.

He kept going. His eyes bulged. His nose spat leakage, over stubble and fringe, sweat, his fatness and chin.

I interrupted him. He obviously wasn't used to being interrupted. I told him again, he was just echoing someone else, word and voice, spit and message, but he didn't understand. I don't think he'd ever read before. He wasn't very good with language.

I asked if he had any kids. A daughter.

I asked if I could talk to her. He said I could.

"What's her name?"

He yelled up the stairs. I found out. She was small, she had a small face, and her aura was small. I walked to the side of the house and they followed me. If she hadn't been so small, she might have been attractive. For some reason it seemed like she was scared of me. I've never thought of myself as being intimidating before. I asked if he understood what the poem meant. He said he didn't know.

:::::::::::::::::::::

We heard a siren from out front roaring. Two cars pulled onto the lawn. People took off running: transformation into an escaping wave. She pulled away, all lips and breath, moonlit beauty, light from inside the house, hair sweeping back. A gust of wind blew.

(She pulled away. *A gust of wind.*)

We ran into the woods. The party fragmented like a star. It was dark here, where the forest made a boundary, through brush and foliage, rustling leaves, rain breaking in the canopy; and vision split. Her hair caught on a branch, but I untangled her. We came out the other side, knelt to catch our breath. She let me borrow her hand. It was still cool.

"You okay?"

Her arm bled, a trailing drop. It got washed off in the rain. She said yeah, ragged, leaning into me. I held her. She sighed. The night danced on her lips. When it was for her, the night could dance. She was real poetry: for her every bow bent, every corner turned. We didn't need supplicants, and we didn't need love. Every light blazed, every star shined. It didn't matter that they'd come for us. We were already gone.

:::::::::::::::::::::

Voices

Writing slow in a hard place, sleeping
twice in the yard. They carry
burnt sticks and hard irons.
The wind carries the scent
of seashells and brine.

::::::::::::::::::::::

"Shit!" I pulled away.

"What?"

"I forgot my camera," I said. "I forgot my fucking camera!"

"Won't you...?"

"No... no I don't think I will."

We stood for a moment. It would be raining soon. No, it was raining already, and it had been raining ever since we left. Two guys came out, looked around, ran in the opposite direction. One of them fell. We still heard the sirens. I took a step toward the forest.

"Wait." She grabbed my hand.

Wait.

And then we were kissing again, bark and limbs, backing her against the tree. We kissed. Her breasts against my chest, full, pressing, she was my winding trail, banking starlit eyes, beautiful, beautiful we kissed. Again, pulling away and: kissing, full bruising lips, stretching and straining, hips and thighs. Pressure.

She did.

We tore.

::::::::::::::::::::::

I ran back through the forest. I might have fallen. The night rushed: the sky and wind. She was waiting for me. She waited. To think once, never so inclined to making gains, inclines and vibes, her sense of the wondrous, to hold her more. If it were just that we had no need to be. If I could stop time there would be no reason to fly.

::::::::::::::::::::::

"What *could*
it mean," he asked. "These kids don't think, these kids don't know. There's no respect in the world." There's no respect.

 I turned
to his daughter and she shook her head. Jacob was right. She didn't understand either.

 "Well,
thanks a lot," I said. "Thanks. You guys were a lot of help. Really."

 I

 left.

 They
hadn't

 helped
at
all
.

::::::::::::::::::::

On the way out, I broke their mailbox.

::::::::::::::::::::

"Jacob, what are you doing here?"

 He looked at me. Pitiful eyes. He didn't belong at this party. I'd already talked to him, small and fearing, no point to making him sway. The gruel never did flow for him, the crows never flew. He was a spider minus webbings, pitiful, pitiful lies, taking advantage, making a home where he didn't belong. We didn't want him here. He hogged more than his percentage of the light.

 "What do you mean?" looking up. "I've got just as much right to be here as you do. You know that. They have a place for me here, and a way for me to be." He nodded once, bobbing. I thought again that I never should have helped him, but he already knew.

::::::::::::::::::::

Voices

On the way
      out,
I broke
   their mailbox.
        It
        cracked,

and the top
caved in, all

   shattered and breaking
in half.

I hate
   that fucking
      guy

    .

::::::::::::::::::::

We kissed
   on the veranda. It was her arms and mine, sanctified: soft smooth skin, running hands down her back, running them up. The night didn't call to us, because the night couldn't call, but we were there and we were really there. She tasted like something that wasn't moonlight. Scent and oranges, color, ellipsoid racing, we kissed. It started to rain. She didn't pull away. The rain matted her hair to us, a fall of water. We kissed. Her essence and the rain, gorgeous,
   she didn't
   pull away.

::::::::::::::::::::

"Are you coming back?" She held onto my hand. She was very beautiful. Incandescence lit her, accenting cheekbones, set and stature, the glow of her, in sight. She stood and the world circled. She was more things than one. She held existence together.
   "Yeah," I said. "I just need my camera."
   "Why?" As she spoke, the sirens got louder. Maybe she could stay. More kids came running. There'd only been two cars. They probably weren't chasing.

"I just need my camera," I said. "It's really important."
"Why?"
She asked again, but right now, it was too much to explain.

:::::::::::::::::::::

On t he
wa y o ut,

I fin all y
br oke

th at
gu y's

fuck ing
mail box.

:::::::::::::::::::::

I talked to Markus again finally. He said he was trouble again, man, he really was. He didn't understand but he was having trouble. He scratched himself once on the face but *it didn't itch* he said he scratched himself again *but it still didn't itch*. He was seeing spiders on the walls and he couldn't even bring himself to watch TV.
—What is it?
—I don't know.
—What is it?
—I've been hearing voices.

:::::::::::::::::::::

Jacob vomited soon, I saw, though I was done paying him attention. I found Markus in the corner and he handed me something to drink. He smelled like smoke. He shook. Permeation, an orangish hazish hazing, hanging in fits, the ceiling, a hazing blanket. I didn't really want to be there. I gave him the drink. I went outside.

:::::::::::::::::::::

Voices

I found
her there, fulminating darkness, iodine imbalance. She sat alone on something that
might have been a veranda, swinging feet, looking around. She sat. I saw her there.
Sight in the dark, I took steps because she'd finally been
found.
—What's up? I said. I saw you today. In the hall, walking the other way. I saw you.
           —I saw you too, she said. I'd already forgotten your name.
       —That's fine. There were people in the way.
       —Yeah, she said. There were people.

:::::::::::::::::::::

"Will you wait for me?" I asked.
       "What?"
       "I just have to get my camera."
       She stood against the tree. The sirens got louder.
       "Yeah," she said. "I'll wait."

:::::::::::::::::::::

"It's starting to rain," I said, and it had. Water clung to her skin, clinging clear and
pure. I kissed her again. "We should probably go inside."
       "Yeah," she said. "We probably should."
       I kissed her again.
                   We never
       went inside.

Markus walked all over the room. He looked up, scratched his face (nervously), and said a prayer too quiet for language. The ceiling fan flung; the floor stayed flat; he could jump up once and never touch the walls. His hair plastered itself; the room stayed silent. We breathed, but of course we breathed. His hamster made hamster sounds, sounding remarkably like a hamster. His mom turned on the vacuum.

"Are you going to be okay?" I asked.

"They're back." He scratched his face, covered in pink streaks; his freckles; worry and fear. "They're everywhere" He shook his head. "They're *every*where..."

"I'm not sure yet," I said. "But maybe."

Outside a car pulled into his neighbor's garage. I stood up, thought of other places we could be. Markus wiggled his foot.

In the those other places

::::::::::::::::::::

we found James throwing rocks at cars. He hadn't hit any yet. I think the idea was to flirt with damage, cracking windshields, a soaring stone. But he wasn't ready to cross the line yet. Pebbles fell short, tires pulled past. He stood too far away. Markus and I threw a few. We missed. We had to miss. We were obligated to miss.

::::::::::::::::::::

Yeah, he said, I know her. She has dark eyes and raven hair? I met her at a party a year or so ago, outside. She was a little drunk. Her boyfriend was in the other room. We talked for a while about Pythagoras and breaking clouds- no, not really, we talked about airplane bathrooms and clubhouses outside the Aegean Sea. I couldn't

Voices

stop staring at her shoulder. We drank a gallon of water together. Her boyfriend never left the other room. She'd acted in a movie, once, she told me, and she could almost play guitar. We kissed a few times. I'm sure I had bad breath. For some reason we never left the table. Her jeans were torn at the knee, and I kept staring at that too. When I told her a story about my mom it made her laugh. She'd never been out of the country before.

::::::::::::::::::::

I found Jacob in his spot again. The dregs were his den of confinement, and the skeletons made room for him there. He wouldn't look me in the face anymore, focusing once on his toes, then memorizing the wall. He sat with his back against the dumpster, leaning, and his head against it too, greased around the edges, a generation of waste. Maybe there were spiders, but there are worse things than venom.

"What do you come here for?" I asked, though I didn't want an answer. I should ask why *I* came. This wasn't my place, I didn't belong here either. *Stains leaked in fear. Puddles did the unmentionable.*

He didn't answer, just shrugged, and stuck one hand in his pocket. His sweater was gray. There were holes in it. Why did he come here, and why did he lay, to sit so silent in the aftermath, alleys, virulent corners? The embers didn't fire. No one wept for him. Maybe he told himself they wept, but I'm sure somewhere he knew better.

He dropped his cigarette. "I know what you're thinking," he said. "I know, and if you're going to be that way then get away. Just go."

I said I was sorry, but I stayed.

"If you're going to be that way," he struggled, the cobwebs shook. He was a den of spiders, of nesting. "Then just go away," he struggled. And when I didn't he flung his bottle at me, missing. It shattered to shards, fragments and stars, a way of life, a cyanide knowing. He cried, face in cuffs, mittens and holes. I stood until the sobs went away.

When it was done he said I never should have helped him.

I said I already knew.

::::::::::::::::::::

Markus's mother watched lots of TV. All her life she'd been addicted to game shows and the scintillating chorus, commercials, infomercials, drama and sitcoms. She only left the television to vacuum. She vacuumed once a day. It made her feel like she had a purpose, Markus said. If she vacuumed then the world had a use for her, one personalized voice, so she could make a difference by keeping the world clean. But it didn't do any good. She hadn't lived in the real world for a long, long time.

::::::::::::::::::::::

I went to a concert to help myself feel real. It was dark where they were. Loud. I screamed even though no one would hear me, just like they did. Together we were a roaring of voice, absolutely depersonalized, entirely without speech. The light roared too. The spectrum gloried, some meager transcendence. I screamed. They played louder. I couldn't even hear my own voice.

::::::::::::::::::::::

James quit throwing rocks. He still hadn't hit any cars. He had his hat turned around his head for leverage, and he looked like a child of the ghetto. He could have been anyone, everyone, together. Cigarettes fell in piles by his feet, one still steaming, a nicotine graveyard, taste and tar brought together for one momentous union.

"What are you doing this for?" I asked.

He spat once. He missed again. "I'm sure you already know."

"I just want to hear you say it."

"What if I won't?"

"Then I'll ask again."

"What if I lie?"

"I'll know."

He laughed. "You won't know."

"Yeah," I said, "I won't."

::::::::::::::::::::::

"Have you ever heard of the center?" James threw another rock.

I said maybe. Markus had, but he wanted to let James tell the story. I might have known, but the longer this goes on, the more I lose, and the more the world becomes an onslaught of voices, catastrophic, that meld and stipulate,

rescind, cacophonous,

      still roaring, like a falling of the stars,

           white and streaking, to make a waterfall of the heavens, in latitudinous
      descent.

      "Well it's not a microcosm—"

      "Kay."

      "—But it's like a microcosm. A focal point, or something, though not really."
James stuck his hand in his pocket, and spat again. "It's like the Holy Grail," he said,
"but at the same time, it isn't. And it's like Pandora's box, but that's not it either."
Thinking. "It's like a reflection of the universe scaled down, that you can hold in the
palm of your hand, though really that's just something else it isn't."

      "Why is it called the center?" I asked. "It's not even in capital letters."

      "Why's anything called anything?" James shrugged. "It just is."

      "But that isn't right," I said. "Things shouldn't just *be*. It doesn't work that way.
Not really."

      "I guess it's like all names," James said. "They're all we have."

      I said that was cool, even though it wasn't.

      A few minutes later we left.

::::::::::::::::::::

I found Travis playing basketball again. It was hotter than yesterday. Sweat ran
down him, a languid perspiration. He wore a jersey (like always), and he had a
sweatband on one arm, by the elbow, because he thought it made him look
authentic.

      He missed.

      Occasionally some good form might show through, but it never got past
imitation. He dreamed too much of the showboat's squander, heaving crowds,
cheering, both hands in the air. They loved him. They would talk about him later,
after the game, to drink in his name. He never lost. He was the epicenter of his own
universe, upwelling, a granulose swarming, they loved him.

      We played for a while. I thought about letting him win. He overshot, thrust
underhand, spun the ball behind, lost it, made whirlwind shots that missed
completely. He was never, had never, and would never be any good. Sometimes I
thought he might know that, though I hope he didn't.

      I beat him.

      Every time we play I think of letting him win, but I never have. I guess it's my
duty to be in tune with the world, and (sometimes) I wondered if it was even
possible for him to win. Travis was a statistic in consistency. He had always lost, and

he would continue to lose, until the sky split open, and the rain came flaming, a furnace, of ice and fire, the elements desisting. He was incapable of victory; no life superceded by dreams, not here in the actual, the factual, the genuine.

He asked to play again, and I beat him twice.

:::::::::::::::::::::

—Do you hear them? I asked.
—Yeah, Markus said. They never go away.
Here
we were
    making sandwiches while the TV droned in the next room.
You can't
hear them
        because they never
    go away.

:::::::::::::::::::::

Yeah, he said, *I met her at a party a few years ago. She has darkish hair, longish/shortish that burns red for a second when the light passes over? When I met her I guess she was fighting with her boyfriend. She came to me and she wasn't crying. Her makeup looked right and her hair looked right too. She wasn't crying.*
    We found
    a bedroom away from everyone else. It was dark there, but you could see out the window, and for some reason someone had a fire going. People kept jumping over it. One fell in (I never found out who), but he didn't get burned very bad.
    I opened the door for her and locked it once she'd gone inside. Even when there wasn't any light she was beautiful. The darkness made canals on her face, accentuating her gothic reverberations, silvery flush, a touch of ivory and smoke, ghosting, quinine, unbelievable.
    (She went inside. I shut the door.) We
    were a schizoid digression. We were clashing
            themes, repeating. She
    was my echo in the night. She
        was my receding
                        memory.
            I kissed her first,

Voices

hard enough to bruise her lips, and she kissed me back so hard the next day my lips <u>were</u> bruised. She was soft: she was gentility and softness, sensuality. The moon made flickers around the room, almost as gentle as she was, but there wasn't any moon, so it must have been the stars, even if I'm sure it wasn't.

We kissed

and they were great kisses. She took steps   toward the bed, languid into shadow, a place where the medians breaks, night and day encasing. She pulled and

I followed where she led. To

scintillating night, brightness and

something like what must make the world glow. And

for some reason

I found myself

remembering the day I met

my first crush, when I was first grade, in what was probably a kindergarten class from a time where I thought the whole world was young. No, I realized, the world had never been young, but that didn't matter with her.

She made the world

into so many things, a whole

world of vision, a chorus of voices, repeating and repeating. And

when she pulled me onto the bed she made me realize before that night I'd never seen something beautiful, I'd never seen life, or meaning, but she gave me that, and she gave me so much more.

When

she pulled me onto the bed,

into

all

that

was her, she brought my world

into focus. She made me complete

and for that

I'll never

forget

her

.

::::::::::::::::::::

"If you were a metaphysical object," I asked, "where would you be hiding?"

Markus gave me a strange look. His eyes fluttered. We kept walking. Cars passed, kicking up dust and rubble, stones, sticks, scattered. Trees swayed in the breeze, bent over; gigantic floral apertures, praying to the earth. I kicked a rock. The rock turned as it crumbled.

"I'm not really sure," he said.

"Somehow," I said, "I'm not surprised."

We kept walking

::::::::::::::::::::

until Ashley picked us up. She was pretty, and she had long, flowing brown hair, the gorgeous kind, so I guess her hair wasn't brown anymore, it was *auburn*. Markus had a crush on her, but that wouldn't end well. Ashley only went for athletic guys, the kind Markus wasn't- who could take off their shirts without being embarrassed, and smile without turning her away. Ashley was more expensive than her car. Her aura smelled of hyacinth and ambrosia. She gave us a ride because she owed me. I'm glad we didn't have to walk.

::::::::::::::::::::

> Never
> listen
> to anything
> I say
> because I like
> to
>
> play
>
> with
> words.

::::::::::::::::::::

Voices

I visited Jacob again. I didn't know why I came back. Every time he I saw him he got lower. He pulled his legs in, crumpling, and something in him got less human. He'd become part of the place, brick and mortar, oppressive. When I spoke to him he groaned, oblivious, not drinking this time, or even smoking, though there were bottles by his hand, and a scattering of ashes. He'd become like the steps and the stones, inanimate as the corner.

He moaned

again, tilting his head. Maybe he noticed me. Drool fell past open lips, pooled by his collar. He moaned. The spiders must have him by now: yeah, his hand was a scarred marking of wounds, needles and poison, they'd sunk their fangs in him, they'd made him their king. Pitiful, dirty, he was their aboriginal God, their arachnid mandala of being. He moaned.

"Jacob?" I asked. "You there, dude?" Though I knew he wasn't. He was a husk peeling, his flaking skin, his quivering eyes. The vultures would come for him soon, they would come, hardness to tear strings of flesh, his apathetic fingers. Mercilessness, they were the end for him, they were coming, unfeeling as the sky, putrid and cool, they came.

::::::::::::::::::::::

I visited my neighbor while she knitted. I found her watching TV. It was all the world had left for her: one eye and vision. Age had taken life from her, taken strength and feeling, so it gave her television. Always watching, she knitted (old), with knobby fingers and a crooked nose, and thought: of things the world had taken from her. It hadn't always been like this, she said, though she wasn't sure if it was all life, or just hers, getting caught up in representation. Nothing was real anymore.

Old pictures hung up on her walls, and tapestries. They were faded. Here everything was faded, where the years were. She had pictures of old things, brightly colored banners, triangulating stars, from an era when it was almost possible to escape anonymity. Sometimes I asked her about them, but she never wanted to talk. Her voice would get tight, and she would sob, and she would scream go, just go, it wasn't any of my business where she'd been, what she'd done, just go. Now I hardly asked her anything at all.

"But sometimes," she said, "when the memory hits (glorious, glorious memory), it makes you remember." As she spoke, her fingers weaved, making the needles move. "I've been alive so much longer than you have, but I feel younger than you do. You don't understand what it means to be alive, you're still too caught up in living. But it passes someday," she nodded, "it really does. And then you'll know."

She gestured at her hands, still threading. It was a mechanical motion, habitual. She didn't have to think, and she didn't have to be. This was her new purpose, fading grasp on function. She made socks and sweaters, stockings, blankets and more blankets. First she made them for her family, so they could wear her memory, and then when they stopped taking them (they hadn't worn them at all) she kept them, and now she threw them into the fire, so she could see them die.

She kept a fire going all year round, so her house was always hot. I was never sure why I went there. I'm not sure why I came.

"I hate this, you know." She looked at her hands, getting older. They were very ugly, and useless, but good for knitting. She was cynical and angry; she was an old woman in a forgotten place. Even the ghosts didn't visit her anymore. She hadn't been alive for so long. The heat, the dust, the dying, she had corpse on her breath, and there was nothing left for her here.

"Yeah," I said, "I know." All the while
wanting very badly
    to leave.

::::::::::::::::::::

My neighbor was bitter, and she hated me.
I was young. She could never forgive me for that.

::::::::::::::::::::

I

   don't go
        to concerts
   anymore.
          They
   suffocate
      me.

::::::::::::::::::::

Voices

"She's so beautiful." Markus leaned forward, taking a drink. He drank orange soda because he said it matched his hair. He had red hair, it wasn't quite orange but it was red if you understood language. Behind him a girl almost as attractive as Ashley came in, walking to the counter. The guy working there was probably her boyfriend. She wore short shorts (a compound meaning), and she never looked Markus's way.

"Yeah," I said, "I guess she is."

He looked at me strange. "You don't think so?"

"I never said that."

"But you just did, didn't you."

"You're just getting caught up in inflection."

I paused for a second.

Sometimes I could be better at feeling. I'm more things than one, and I don't understand what it means to subliminify. It's gone beyond the point of trust. I'm too fond of making up meanings.

"Where did you meet her?" he asked.

"You know where."

"But why do you know her?"

"You know that too."

He sighed, and sat his drink down again, fizzing. He said I shouldn't be right so often.

I am.

::::::::::::::::::::

Travis wanted a rematch.

::::::::::::::::::::

James threw another rock. He missed; he always missed; he was obligated to miss. Markus hung back. He picked up a strand of grass, twining until the filling bled. I stood. A cloud passed by. The sky was higher than we were. Most likely this would never change.

::::::::::::::::::::

"Hey Ashley," I tapped her on the arm. Markus gave her appreciative looks. "Don't go this way." She asked why and I'm sure Markus wanted to answer. I almost let him.

She smiled. Her lips were wide, full, dark, luscious. All sorts of words that have nothing to do with vision. She was an ostentatious, prettyful lie, and she might have been the most beautiful girl in the world.

I bet Markus wanted to touch her hair. Maybe, if she was in a good mood, she would let him.

::::::::::::::::::::

"James is throwing rocks at cars," I said.
"Oh," she said, and went another way.

::::::::::::::::::::

"So where did you meet her?"
"School."
"Did you become a single person in two bodies?"
"Only once."
"How long ago?"
"A long time."

The girl with the legs was still at the counter. She was unreal. Her legs were too dark for nature, and she was too naked to be human. We're all the same underneath, or so they say. I pointed her out to Markus. He stared for longer than I did.

"Was it before you met *her*?" I loved the way he enunciated, pronunciated, droned. She wasn't quite ripe for capitalization, but there might be a day, someday.

"It was a long time ago. Before."
"You realize, right, that you might never find her again?"
"I realize."

He sighed again, and finished the rest of his drink. Ice cubes clinked to the bottom, absolutely without purpose. If he set them outside they would evaporate soon. The streets and the city didn't care: useless and impotent, melting.

"Sometimes," he said, "I think I might be better off you than are."

::::::::::::::::::::

Voices

—Was she there when you got back? he asked.
I was too afraid to answer.

::::::::::::::::::::

(why,
didn't
you leave?)

::::::::::::::::::::

Yeah, he said, *I met her at a party a few years ago. She had darkish reddish hair that got bluish when the light hit it right, over every strand, illuminating? I met her once. She didn't say anything about a boyfriend. She came up to me all angles and elbows and cheekbones and graceful shoulders. She blew me*
    in the hall. I was surprised too. We were just making out, then she had her hand on me and I was on the floor and people were walking past some of them maybe giving us strange looks if they realized what we were doing. She was my nymphomaniac vulture, striking, with violent beauty, with willowy, flowing fingers, her nubile tongue. full, full. lips. I've
    never been so surprised before. Not since once when I was young and I discovered that if you try sometimes you really can get away with lying if no one knows if you don't give yourself away so soon. She gave me restraint and cardiac arrest, a paradise that didn't so often have to lie. But the strangest thing
    was that when she was done (the people still passing, giving us strange looks, her splayed hair and horizontal posture) I felt dirty, or used. No. that wasn't true. I'd used. her.(she.was) my ticket to purity. But it didn't matter. I couldn't help thinking that she'd used me, by being so perfect, by never coming back. I think I still might love her. I've never dealt with loss
    very well.

::::::::::::::::::::

Birds flew by overhead, aerodynamic, a flock of prophets, changing seasons. No: the winter wasn't coming soon, no ice, no falling snow. If they shat, then they shat, and Markus would eat shit, in his nose and mouth, white and falling, putrid, hardening. The seasons changed. The year was not ending. James threw more rocks.

"You know, dude," I said, "if you keep this up long enough, sooner or later you really are going to hit a car."

He shrugged.

"I know."

::::::::::::::::::::

I found him again: Jacob in his cave, where the world fell away. No wind blew, not wasting in the alley. All was stagnant as an empty night in a dead city, where the corpses were, where death, and rot, and enmity came awake.

"Why do you come here?" he asked. There were cracks on his skin, and spiders, making webs to anchor him to the wall. His eyes were the dullness of inhumanity, lidless, unseeing. I don't think he could move. His sweater had many holes. Redness strung his face and hands, strings of infection, sickness and hurt. He wept. He was a monster and a horror, weaping for lost life, distant memory and gross, gross pain.

"If you want," I said, "I could help you."

"You've done enough."

"Maybe I have." I turned my back on him. He was hideous, disgusting and vile. He smelled of old flesh, fermentation, mucus, filmy. The insects had not been kind to him. They were parasites of the very worst, burrowing, pecking his pieces. I turned around.

"If you want," I said, "I could still help you." Though I didn't want to, and I didn't think I could. There was no leaving this place, no forgetting awful transformation. He took a croaking, groaning breath and spat yellow, wormy phlegm. It had roaches in it. He didn't move. Slime stuck him to the wall behind. I couldn't bare to see.

"I know what you're thinking," he said.

"What's that?"

"You're thinking about what it means to approach geometric patterns as though they were art." He coughed. "And how difficult it is to tell red from dark red, red orange from something in the middle. That is," his voice broke, and he didn't sound like him anymore. "That is what you're thinking about, isn't it?"

"It was."

"And you're thinking you never should have helped me."

"Maybe."

"Get out of here," one last time. "If you're going to be that way. I don't want you here, and I don't want you seeing me like this." He was crying, yeah if he could cry, acid, venomous tears.

"I can't go yet," I said.

Voices

"You can," he said. "Yes you fucking can." Groaning.
     You   *did*
                              this to me.
I shook my head.
"You did this to yourself," I said, "and you know
                              that
                              too."

    "Just get out," he said.
I

went.

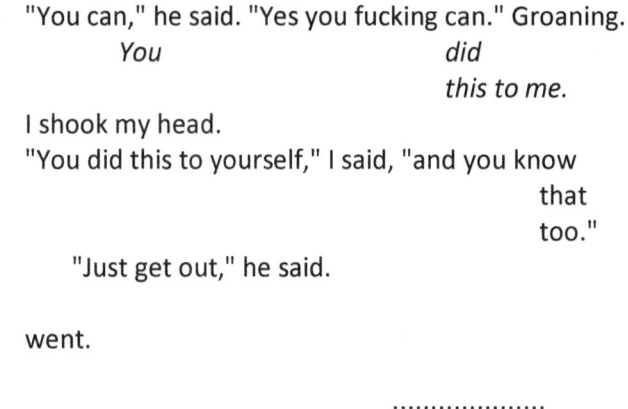

::::::::::::::::::::::

Markus's mother was a prophet of cereal box wisdom, new prescriptions and popular opinion. She preached to us. We learned very little. She knew her images, her falsehoods and prejudices. On occasions she got very passionate. Just as frequently I tended to walk out. Somewhere inside, I hope she understood why.

::::::::::::::::::::::

The next time Travis asked me to play, I decided to let him win. He tried very hard. He went half an hour without making one shot. It got to the point he couldn't even dribble. The ball flew from him at unrealistic angles, warping physics, deflected oddly, playing strange directional games. Half an hour later we were still zero to zero. He gave up, congratulating me on a game well dominated, leaving to go home.
    It feels good to be right.

::::::::::::::::::::::

I finally talked to that prostitute after years of seeing her there.
    When I was young, I think I might have been in love with her, but I'm not sure. I'd seen her one day, when I was walking to school, and dreamed about her later. I didn't know what it meant to like a woman; she was just a mysterious thing, pretty, wild and pretty, with her dark hair, her crazy angles.
    She's almost thirty now, but still pretty. I'm not sure what I saw in her, but she was a multitude of things, spanning an individualized past, unfathomable.
    We went into an alley. She stuck her hand down my pants. When I said I didn't want sex she looked at me strangely. What was I there for, she asked, if I didn't want sex? I said I wanted to meet her, vulnerable in her absence of self, respect and

center. If I paid her, she would let me do anything. I didn't want her to be an object. She said it was all she knew how to be.

"I just want you to talk to me," I said.

"That's the thing," she said. "I don't know how."

::::::::::::::::::::

"Can you hear them now?" I asked.

"You sound like a commercial."

"It doesn't matter," I said. "We all sound like commercials."

"I suppose that's true."

I wondered if there should be a question mark there.

There I was, being imperative, being interrogative: man and creature, stealer of souls. No, that's not true. If we had souls the world must have had them already, swirling, a glorious brocade of screaming, screaming voices, onto a brutal, impious sense of the grand, the great, the final.

Markus waited. He said he couldn't hear, though he might have been lying.

"What about you?" he asked.

Maybe.

We walked. Cars passed, a convalescence of faces, grilles and glowing eyes, not living. We'd been here before, to find the center, making war on whispers. We left behind a trail of paper cups, gum wrappers and footprints. They. we left behind. Tw.igs. leave.s. the breaking. Times.

"Why won't you ever give me an answer?" Markus asked.

"Because I'm an enigma."

"That's bullshit."

"I know."

We kept going. Behind, the road snaked to the fading point, crooked, a stretched, broken finger, asphalt and distance, driven. We weren't vehicles, not waiting anymore.

"Yeah," I said, "I hear them."

::::::::::::::::::::

Voices

"You could just talk to her, you know."

    Markus shook his head, cringing. I knew somewhere inside he wanted to, but he never would, and I knew that too. He was afraid, and he had always been afraid. Most likely he would never be within a few feet of her again. I wasn't nice enough to tell him the hard way, but at least this way I looked like a friend.

.

.

.

I didn't
       feel
            like walking
                 anywhere.

::::::::::::::::::::

Yeah, he said, *I know her. I can't describe her anymore than anyone else can, but I know her. I met her at a party a few months ago, in the back room, and we talked for a long time. She had interesting things to say. I haven't met an interesting girl since, and most likely, I'd never met one before either. She didn't say anything about a boyfriend, but I was too scared to ask.*

    It's not true, you know, what they say about her. They tell stories because no matter what she'll always be there, but the stories they tell aren't true. About bedrooms at midnight, about hallways? She told me none of them were true, and I believe her. If I didn't believe her, she said, no one ever would.

    We talked for a long time. We sat on a table, kicking things. I gave her my drink. Halfway through I told her I loved her, though she wouldn't say anything back. We were silent for a few minutes. She was a bringer of silence, a prophet of radiance. People don't understand the light she gives off. If the world could circle her, then it would. And there's a chance it does already.

    When we finished, I realized the party was already over. I stepped on a few people on the way out. I got her another drink. She said she didn't need a ride home. If she had, I would have given it to her. She said thanks, and it was the first time I've ever cared for gratitude. Before she left, she gave me a hug. I'd never cared for hugs before either.

::::::::::::::::::::

James threw harder this time. He threw hard and I already knew. It cut an arch through the sky, air-shaped, that undid ancient theories of propulsion. It flew, I'd already known. Author of meanings, bringer of prophesy. Molecules wavered, making room, and boundaries shattered like cracking glass.

The car swerved off the side of the road. It fell in a ditch. The rock scratched a crevice over the windshield, stark white on cleanliness. The car spat black smoke, an emblem of damage.

"We should probably get out of here," I said.

We did.

Voices

I

...they can

(echo)

Kyle Muntz

Voices

Sometimes
 I wonder if it really isn't an issue of time and place, of derangement, of blinking. Those are days I sit on an old tire and throw rocks into trashcans. Those are the boring days, the wasting days, the silent moments. My friends tell me I'm not the same anymore, but I don't think they understand change. If I've changed, then I obviously don't need sameness.
 I've never been fond of magicians. They're just extremely talented liars who are far, far too good at what they do. I don't think people
 understand that
 either.

::::::::::::::::::::

"What's your name?"
 We were in the alley again, and it was dark here. Spilled trash, rotten onion, hydrogen peroxide, lubricating oil. Hidden spots are microchasms of waste. They don't smell very good either.
 "It's Veronica," she said. Her hair spilled wild, an auburn cascade, her sense of European distinction; she was all jagged angles and emphasis, not an accessible beauty, not a face to pass by. She wore red today, or crimson, though it was crimson, with the context she gave it. I never understood how she could walk in heels, advertising herself- but no, they didn't care for that, she was all surface contours and flair, to catch the eyes, to the anchor the gaze. Sometimes I wondered if it was possible to love her, but it wasn't much of a question.
 We talked for a
 while.

I had trouble following the conversation, its flow and curvature, fragmentary. There we were, dualistic, rebounding voices, alone in a dark place where none but the highest lights shone.

"Where are you
from?"
not, "here."
It's not difficult hating this place, but even
harder to love it.
"Were you born,"
here?
I've never
really understood birth. "No
it's not" a matter
of renewability either, just
I

had trouble following the conversation. A while in she told me, that maybe, if I hadn't been buying her time, she might have given it to me anyway. I said thanks, though I've never been liberal with gratitude. We stood together in the alley, drifting together, drifting away. Then we sat on opposite sides, facing together, where I could see up her skirt. I wasn't sure if she did it on purpose. She had long, long legs. She was a goddess of vision, and she was easy to love.

::::::::::::::::::::

I went to a poetry reading and met revelation there. I've never been fond of personification, but sometimes poetry personifies itself. Sometimes personality *itself* is impersonal. Transformation is pointless without mediums.

I met a kid named Jacob there. That's not true. I'd met him before, but seeing him made me remember. I didn't like him immediately, or remembered immediately, that I didn't like him. He had a sallow face and rotten teeth. He was hateful, spite and wrongness, casting no shadow. The light didn't touch him well. He took up too much space. But at the same time, too little.

The world doesn't drink poetry. There were maybe four of us. We didn't even get free coffee. I tried. They said they'd give me ten percent free, and they didn't even give me that. But at least they had something like a stage. If you spoke loud enough, maybe you might be heard.

None of the poetry was any good. It didn't have any personality, flair, verbosity. It was just stuff about leaves and bristles, May mornings in young homes where the

Voices

sun beats *shining* through the window huge yellow fire: you look out smiling think (maybe) this might be something akin to peace. They made frequent, failing use of the alphabet, rhyming poorly like old, dead men, and painfully, like children telling lies. No real poet invents truth. The truth, unfolding, reinvents itself.

::::::::::::::::::::::

At times, I can be wildly, wildly opinionated.

::::::::::::::::::::::

Markus was right. Ashley couldn't have been more attractive. The invisible centered on her, and she captured attention without knowing. They all knew her, and I did too, possibly as much as they did, by looking at her, contemplating fantasy. She was an endlessness of fantasy, unknowable. The unrecognized, the petty.

Markus told me he liked her. He like her then, and he would always like her. She was a motif of the oblivious, a grandiose messenger of the painful. Markus didn't understand what I meant. No one seemed to. I thought of saying more, but I didn't know either, any more than he did. She was illusive, invisible, a savior. No, she wasn't, would never, and had never been a savior, but she looked like one, and she

saved.

"I hope you're less intimidating than you look," I said.

She shrugged and said maybe she was. She said it intimidatingly.

Liar.

::::::::::::::::::::::

It wasn't fun to write poetry in the park- there where wind blew, where the flowers bloomed, nature's artifice in the city. There wasn't enough energy: too many people, barking dogs, drops of rain. Grass fell over, beaten unreal. Maybe a long time ago there might have been water in the fountain. There still was, but you never know.

All my life, never wanting to feed the birds. I'm no thrower of bread, not a shower of manna. I threw anyway. I wrote poetry no one understood. People came here to reclaim the old life. Old.

"Hey."

I looked up. Someone's figure blocked out

the sun. They were new. They were some fabulous, foreign
presence, blocking
(out)
the sun.

"Hey," as though I could speak, more than a sound, a syllable, an artifice. I
wondered if this mystery understood language (and through it, if they understood
the world). They weren't gender, they weren't memory and a cognoscente kind of
feeling. I wondered how soon
        that would change.

"What's your name?"

      "I'm not sure."

And there I was with a laughing mystery. Time and place, setting, flow and a
direction in the light. Fine. I looked down, my shoe, I saw it, cracks in the pathway,
trees in the distance, ants and anthills, bicycles- the bars still on them- taxi(the
blinking lights!)'s, little kids and their parents, blankets, bedlam, fried chicken and a
handsomely carved ham sandwich.

"Do you remember me?"

"Not really."

Good. You probably shouldn't. We've never met.

I figured.

Good. "So what's your name?"

I already told you.

Right.

      He stepped out of the light. Already
he'd become less of a mystery. I wasn't sure what that meant: graduation,
accumulation, percolation of beating message; iron, iron, iron. I kicked over a
cardboard box. A dog rolled over. Something moved in the trees.

         You
want a camera? he asked.

If you offered me one, I'd take it.

I'm
      offering.

Then
I'll
    take it.

(something splintered in the backings.)

Voices

...
I've
been hearing
      voices.

::::::::::::::::::::

"How did I do?" I asked.

Jacob shook his head, wiped a finger on his face. Disgusting. He smelled like urine and unripe cheese.

"You did okay," he said, "just..."

"Just what?"

"No one understands what you're talking about," he said. "You just... I guess you need to be clearer, or something. And vomit isn't poetic. Neither is sex.

Not like that."

"But I didn't write about sex, or vomit."

"It seemed like you did."

"I thought you didn't understand?"

"I understood enough.

"I don't think you do," I said. And

he obviously

didn't,

      though

                  I don't know why

      he thought

      he

did.

::::::::::::::::::::

Where are you from? I asked. We were in the alley again, if we'd ever left. Very few people walked past. The dust made us invisible.

      I thought
I already told you?

You weren't telling the truth.

Veronica shook her head. *Yeah,*
she said, *you're right, I*
wasn't.

        Why
        not?

Because
I don't like thinking
about where I come
from.
        She
        laughed,
                spread her legs
a little,
        looked
        at me and said,

        The first thing
        they tell you
            when
        you start out, just a scared
little girl, homeless
and alone, sitting there
with both legs crossed in front of you, feeling
        worthless and vulnerable,
        (knowing they'll fuck
        you soon, just to test you
        out,
because they've got
hard, hungry dicks
        and
        lust to fill you with)
        is that
        you aren't a person anymore; you aren't
a real girl, who smiles and makes people care, gives a
look and
changes lives. With you

men can be animals again.
You don't
cry late at night,
and you don't care to be respected.
No one
respects an object, so
try not
to feel anymore.
It's easier that
way.

She looked up. She
might
have been crying.

All I can do," she said,
is take their
advice."

::::::::::::::::::::::

I saw James on the street. He looked the same as always, with his hat on backwards, clothes a few sizes too big. Seeing back, he waved. We went the same direction, with the flow of traffic, converging. The world had fingers. It reached out for us: grasping.

"Have you ever heard of the Chimera?" he asked.

"Like... is it a monster?" I said. "I know about monsters."

But he said it wasn't, shaking his head. Amazement gave him expression, a new kind of thinking, whereby his lips got thinner, and his eyes started to bulge. Walking carelessly, he'd run into three people since we'd met up. They turned angry, but he didn't care. He lived in his own world, everywhere at once. It was a scary place, where he lived.

"I'm not really sure how true this is," he said.

"That's fine."

"It's this kid," James said. "I don't know what he looks like, or if he even exists, but I guess he can control time and space. You know, like a God, or something. Time and space." He raised a hand and made a fist, impressively. "Isn't that awesome?"

he said. "He's like a superhero or something. No, not a superhero, even cooler. He's that piece of the real that just shouldn't be. He's a new kind of ultimate."

"Think I'd be able to meet him?"

James stopped. "I don't think he's really the kind of guy you *meet*." He paused. "He's supposed to be like a myth, that's what gives him his power. That's not a system you fight. It's dangerous."

"I know," I said, "but it's fine, I'm a fighter."

"No you're not."

"Yeah, you're right, I'm not."

We walked silently. It's never silent in the city, but we ignored the details. Here was a den of advertisement, of inequity. I wanted a fine, fab-ulous cheeseburger.

"If I was going to get in contact with him," I said, "how do you think I'd do it?"

James took off his hat and wiped his forehead, obviously thinking I was insane. "I dunno," he said. "I think you just *do.* If you want to meet him, he'll know. He always knows. He's the Chimera."

"When do you think it'll happen?"

"When he wants it to."

Measuring footsteps, I supposed that made sense.

::::::::::::::::::::::

I saw her in class. Ashley had presence. I asked her once if she knew she had presence and she said she did. It was something apart from what she was. She didn't know it, and she had never known it, but she knew. Secret, a sacred kind of knowledge, I could barely even see it anymore.

"Do you have secrets?" I asked.

"Of course I do," she said.

(That's good. I was just making sure.)

"You should tell me one," I said. "I'm good at keeping secrets."

She giggled. Maybe, on some level, she might have trusted me.

"Meet me after class," she said.

"Where?" I asked.

"You know where."

And I realized I did, though sometimes knowledge is hard to explain.

::::::::::::::::::::::

Voices

I

I met her
there after class, but of course she wasn't alone. Ashley was never alone, because everyone is always thinking of her. I met her there, not alone; she made me her keeper of secrets. There were two of her, and she was in love with herself. She looked gorgeous, and she looked gorgeous together. She touched, keeping secrets, here where the teachers never came, where secrets kept.
I saw her there, touching
with herself. I couldn't tell. With Ashley you can never tell. She kept her own secrets, by being so beautiful, by staying her own. Maybe, just maybe, she might have been real. She didn't
feel lust, she didn't feel hurt or forsaken. In hiding, she hid, to play games with belief, to play games, not a real secret at all. If she'd been less than herself, I might have
cared.   II

I met
her there. It wasn't an issue of time or place, but maybe I could make it one. If this was where we were, then(III)
maybe I've been talking to the walls. We pressed against the walls. She felt more real than a real woman. Her skin too smooth to be real, giving off no heat, she was all restraint and coolness, the quixotic stranger, riding naked into the sunset, her glorious silhouette, teasing with well, well sculpted shoulders. Water dripped down, to puddle gently, florid crispness, ripeness and flowers, a temperate afternoon in parts of the city where the night   never comes, sitting outside, decorating the curb and watching the cars go by, the suits and ties, briefcases, schoolbags. We
did kiss, and it was the most unreal kiss of my life. I didn't know if Ashley was meant to be touched. I'd never heard of her being real before. Markus knew the real her, the personification of her: chords, notes on the vibraphone. She was nothing like a jazz café in the nineteen seventies, drinking cocktails while the day melted, the saxophone bled, and she wasn't like the postal service either, who bring packages, who deliver envelopes, though she brought things. Without
getting caught up in innuendo, I can't
say much can

in fact
say very little. I promised to keep her secrets, I promised to be that one, true
release, if that's anything like what I was. If I told what
it meant to be with her I can't say. If I
pretended to think honestly I'd just be going back to more innuendo. In breaking
my promise, all I can say was it was unreal. She was unreal, breathing. I knew
what it means to keep secrets, and I knew more things than that, reaching, in my
own way, all across vast, cyclic realms of the symbolic wheel, echoing voice... She
was full of surprises, she was capable of being naked. I wondered if this was
anything like the real her, if you could call it that, not just
another element of what it means to be human, representative of the race, the
human species, who do lust, even when they hide it behind alien symbiosis, latching
onto etiquette, her wildness, something resembling IV
She
was full of surprises, but the most surprising thing,
was that she came
first.

::::::::::::::::::::

One

reason

                        art
          can only
imitate
                  life
                  (without
recreating)
is that
                  it
          doesn't capture
those moments
          in
          between.
(though sometimes

Voices

```
        there
                    isn't
                    much reason
    to
        try.)
```

::::::::::::::::::::

"If anyone asks," Ashley said, "make sure you tell them we did it once."
   "I thought I was keeping secrets."
She laughed, and might have smiled.
   "I don't have secrets," she said. "You know that."
I said I didn't want to quit pretending.
   "We never quit pretending," she said. "You know that too."
   I kissed her again. Her lips didn't taste real. Like painted plastic, they were full and fuller, but she never stopped pretending.

::::::::::::::::::::

I had a dream the day before I met *Her*. She'd gotten to the point of capital letters (not to mention *italics*). I woke up (dreaming), in a place where the canals were, under a bridge (I woke in a dream). Beams of light shot through crevices, knifing brighter than belief, and lit a furnace of illumination: cracks, crevices, lichens, underneath the water, a rigorous sea of brightness. There might have been people (I heard their steps, quickly passing), but I couldn't see them, though for some reason they wore robes, yeah, they must have been wearing robes.
   I followed the water. All my life I've been good at following things, because I'm a person, and somewhere deep inside I like direction. Instead I followed brightness, not flickering, solidness, a luminescent body, and I found her there, a girl I didn't know. Transfiguring, she didn't have a real, permanent face, a true, rigorous self. She just was, and she was everything else too, all at once.
   "What's your name?" I asked.
   When she wouldn't tell, I wasn't surprised.

::::::::::::::::::::

Veronica looked different today, less like herself, in that she wasn't so there, and she wasn't wearing heels. When I showed up she tasted me tentatively, the way you kiss a stranger, no the way you kiss a friend. Scents, she smelled like expensive perfume, essence of the rain.

"I missed you," I said. I did. But what was. She gave me nothing to deny. She was herself, but she was easy to love. Distinguished, mysterious, she kept her own secrets. Therefore, to who I am, keeper of knowing.

If you want, she said, we could make a video.

She bent her head, and leaned against the wall. Her angular hips, the set of her, feline, delirious, strenuous, she reminded me of adolescent lusts, of the earliness of memory, thinking of her. All my life I'd been keeping secrets, no, just a kind of individual knowledge, of myself, that she let me preserve. Dark markings accented her, lash and pupil, denouncing vision. If I asked, maybe we could run away together, to an oasis in the desert where water cools the flames... she could be my desert oasis, haunting spiritualist dream. Not that which I know, all that was she. Weakness, beauty, we could run away to the desert, and bathe in perfect, perfect flame, scouring, a tempestuous sun- devouring- streams to set free... If she'd asked I would have gone, I knew, we could keep secrets someplace away from this city (streets, cafés) where no one understands poetry. If she asked we could go... we might have gone.

"If you want," she said, "we could make a video." She asked the wrong questions. No, she just didn't ask the same way, assaulting, refraction: thinly, making slopes and shapeliness, a band of skin below her shirt. I'd never realized she was taller than I am. I could touch her, maybe I could, feeling, she would let me. Was that it, really, what it meant to diffuse into her, she making returns, an energetic linkage. I relinquished vision. It remembered her.

I didn't have to see up her skirt anymore. We made our own vision of loveliness. She let me touch her. I didn't have to pay.

::::::::::::::::::::

The city never sleeps. Sometimes I feel like I don't belong here, where even the natural is made of plastic. Dissonant, distance and misrepresentation. I couldn't sleep. I clung to the idea of being an enigma, but the world didn't have a place for anonymity either. Linkage. A maze of advertisements and hanging black wires.

I met him again in the park, a mystery. Phallic connotations demarked him, something to do with gender perception, linguistic in the social pathos, (deeper than slang and last week's scandal). Dissonant, preconceived, he confused me.

Voices

"You're the one who gave me my camera, right?"

He looked at me strangely, and asked what I meant. I couldn't make out his face. Shadows stretched from brow to the line of the nose. Yellow beams obscured him. Shifting in his seat, maybe he thought about sitting down. He looked back at me. Maybe he knew, what things given, a possession not taken away. I'd never thought of meeting him again, not here in the dark, but passing obscures the prophetic, and bleeds it to dreams.

After standing a moment longer, he said maybe he had.

"Do you have it now?"

I always have it.

A night bird flew. Deranged old men, wielding canes and crooked back walkers, stumbled in the sideways, swearing under their breath, growing patches of hair on their upper lips. The moon hid behind clouds, not looking down on the city. We gave it no rest, a haunting to go on ten million years. Maybe someday I could see the moon, rising up, to make amends for humanity. But nothing comes through that blurring curtain.

"Want to go somewhere?" he asked. "I feel like a trip into the forest."

"But there isn't really a forest there," I said. "They just want it to look like a forest, to keep up appearances, but twenty feet in the trees stop, and you come out the other side. Even nature isn't real anymore."

He said it didn't matter, and dragged me in behind. Tonight, beating that nameless hour, the clock stopped, not spinning in circles, or keeping track of numbers. The grass sung. Wetness crinkled to steps, raining. No wind blew. It was not raining.

We went on a journey through the forest. Thirty feet in the canopy broke. Thick brush masked the path behind. It led nowhere: dark branches, silent, unmoving. The trees were bigger back here, and more real, with nothing scribed in the bark, no place to declare everlasting love. I left my own footprints. They were shaped very much like my shoes.

We went on a journey in the forest.

Inside, darkness swallowed us whole, a thick, hardening darkness, carving caves in nature, lapsing through the real. He might have led. Specters, silent stepping, owls flew overhead with a burst of winds. They hunted because they were less than human. Ferns, still browning, were almost but not quite dead. I felt like washing my hands.

We were travelers in a place where the real never came, nature imitating memory- seeing ghosts, pale-white; with hallow eyes and clear skin. Forgetfulness admonished them, millennia outscored them. If grasshoppers could moan, then they moaned. Moth patches fluttered, netlike. Trees held conversation.

An indigo rift, pulsating, scoured the landscape, smelling heavily of pigmentation and dynamite. It had electricity in it, cackling white and blue. Furious lightning sprung from it, making scars in dirt, trees, and pinecones, lighting purple fires and tearing new holes. Above, the moon shown down, judgmental. It heard very little. The stars were not kind to us.

I went on a journey in the forest, not where I'm going. This wasn't science fiction, and this wasn't a salt-sea mooring romance, killing great beasts from somewhere near the bottom of the world. Blue fire engulfed us. White lightning destroyed us. Whispering, the dryness of spiders, papery along the walls. Melancholy rebuked us. Harmonious music, transcendent, undid us.

I went on a journey in the forest.

::::::::::::::::::::

Jacob spouting nonsense, his stupid fucking adolescent bullshit, regurgitation, stupidity. "I think she's the one. Really, she is."

"That's nice."

"It is," Jacob said. He wrung his hands. "I'm going to ask her to marry me. We could be together forever, we really could." Still wringing his hands.

Someone opened the door. I might have come here for poetry, though more likely I hadn't.

Whatever it was, I hadn't come here for Jacob.

"How long have you been together?"

"A month," he said, "or two."

The sidewalk repeating itself. Existence ran out of ideas. At intersections, reams of exhaust, burping and flooding. The light changed colors. Jacob buried his eyes in the nearest waitress. He was scum; he understood nothing of self-awareness.

"Do you have a ring?" I asked.

He said he didn't. Not yet, at least. But he would. He was getting one from a friend, and it would be really nice, he swore, though he hadn't seen it yet, so he didn't know. "She won't know it's used." He took a drink. "So it's a great idea." He didn't deserve carbonation, or any amount of sodium water. The world had very little use for him.

"If you want," I said, "I'll be honest."

"How so?"

"I could tell you how bad of an idea this was."

Voices

He snorted.

"If you wanted," I said, "I could give you great advice."

"Like what?"

"Take back everything you just said, forget about that ring, and find a nice, quiet corner to be embarrassed at yourself."

Jacob looked down. His upper lip wiggled. He balled his hands to fists.

"What do you know about love?" he asked. "What do you know?"

"Obviously more than you," I said, though when I thought about it later, repeating myself, I started to sound and more like

a liar.

:::::::::::::::::::::

I woke up

in the park,
at
the edge
of the forest, though
somehow everything
felt
more
like a dream
than ever
before.

:::::::::::::::::::::

I talked to an old man in the park, while I wrote a poem about the forest. It was thick/cornerless, a place/where wanderers/went, to find a part of themselves/still living. Though I abandoned it after a few lines, wondering at myself, for writing so horribly. Sometimes I feel like/for all the lines/I've penned, I've never written/anything/truly original... and those are the scary days. I experiment with punctuation because rhythm isn't enough for me anymore. Someday I plan on chasing sentences away.

"When I was young," the old man said, "all this, all around, this city used to be grass and farmland, forests, grazing fields and patches of muskrat ter-ritory, where the gophers lived. Over there," he pointed, with an aged, crooked finger, "there used to be a path, winding, that led to the river, and a forest that went back further, to place no man ever came. Until, that is, he destroyed it.

"Yes," he said, "when I was young, there used to be wilderness here."

"Does it matter?"

He dropped his head to his hands, wrapped them both around his cane. Drooping. I'd never seen someone so old. His hair wisped cloudlike over a wrinkled skull. His clothes were fifty years out of date. All my life, I'd never feared such transformation. But he taught me the meaning of fear, the eventuality of age.

"How would I know?" he exclaimed, angrier than language could make him. "I'm just an old man. My generation didn't care about the past either. The young are always the same." He cackled, frightening in his oldness. "But I have my secrets," he said, "I do. My past, the past I know, is something you can never go back to, and I'll own it forever. I could be lying," he cackled again, "and you would never know."

"You are," I said. "There's never been a forest here."

He looked at me bitterly. It couldn't matter. In remembering, he'd lost himself to something that wasn't the past, glorified, imaginative. The history he knew was a magnification of the internal: embittered. I didn't hate him, but I didn't pity him either. He reminded me of vicious unreality. Even now I'd lost touch, forever, with the real.

::::::::::::::::::::::

"Did you tell them?" Ashley asked.

"Yeah," I said, "I told them. Just once."

She gave me a hug.

"But I have to ask," I said. "Why did you want me to lie?

::::::::::::::::::::::

I met her there. For some reason my life seems to have become a sequence of secret meetings in secrets places normal people don't want to go- or I could put it that way, if I took the past into consideration. I considered the past: classes at the last minute, passing through doorways. Memory gave me difficulty. I felt like I'd separated from myself. Maybe I had.

"Do you..." Veronica touched my shoulder, brushed her fingers away. Still, we were asking the wrong questions. "Do you have anyone?"

One of us was nervous. I might have been projecting myself, playing a game of masks through a mirror.

Voices

Maybe. Maybe I had someone. She would be the first to know.

"I was just wondering," she said, "if you did, that is. Just because. I wondered."

"No," I said, "I don't think... there was another girl, last year, but it wasn't about us, really. So no, I don't think I do."

"Oh," she said. "Oh."

I took her hand. It was longer than mine, slender and cool. She had many skills. She was an artisan of the flesh, a fountain. Our fingers came together. No, this wasn't a time for innuendo. I wasn't a teenage boy telling jokes in smoky places. That, for, was life, was. Could I feel, did I? Thinking back, and feeling, thinking. All I'm good at is playing games with words. The world escapes me.

"I wrote a poem for you," I said. "Has anyone... has anyone ever written a poem for you before?" She said no. She was lying, but I didn't mind. She lied for me, if she was. I knew. I always know. "You want to hear it?" I asked. I hoped she did.
I whispered
the poem in her ear, gently,
as she curled

to me, gently.
    Unfortunately,
    it wasn't as though I could
    just feel her dreams, but I
    felt her, and we felt

            together, something
    powerful, something
    potent
    that might have been love, if we felt
    like calling it names, meditating on connection, purely
    to amuse ourselves. We were children together, the way
    we made each other laugh, gently.
As if we were

        children, and someday we would be young
    again, renewed, gently,

    and we could float in clouds, swim in rainbows,
    if we did it together, metaphorically, together. It wasn't
    a good poem, but I sometimes

      I wonder
if I've ever
    done a good poem, possibly
    it's just I've been thinking in volumes, made,
    past, plated, lines and lines and
    voices.

    I repeated
    myself a bit too often,
and I got bound

    a bit
    by the constraints
    of the medium, but did she notice, I hope
    she didn't notice, because
    if she noticed
    I think I might have started
    to cry, though she didn't,
    and neither
    did I.

::::::::::::::::::::

That's not quite true.
I need to work on my improvisation.
Technically, I've been
getting a bit sloppy,
and there's nothing poetic
about that.

::::::::::::::::::::

"Did you like it?" I asked.

    She said she did.
I knew she cared because she was willing to lie.

    "Come away with me," I said. "We could

Voices

run away to the desert.

<u>Did you</u> understand?

She was
willing
to lie.

:::::::::::::::::::::

"You were right," Jacob said.

            Of course. (he didn't add)

Jacob teetered back. He had dirt between his fingers, a foul stench in him.
He fell.
I thought of catching him, but he fell.
"So what happened?" I asked.
"She didn't like the ring."
"Did you show it to her?"
"No. But she didn't like it. And," (he made strange sounds, like breaking sobs, from somewhere in his bowels, or glutei) "I think she was getting tired of me. Either that or I got tired of her. I don't know. Bitch. I hate her. Bitch." Biting his tongue once, not cringing. "I hate her."
"Did you take my advice?"
"Yeah," he said. "I found a corner. Maybe someday you could visit me there."
"Maybe."

:::::::::::::::::::::

The bridge sprung over sea like a great concrete mouth, linking land and land, a spurning tongue of rock, bearing (well oiled) metal, its stoniness, its silt and foundation. Bits of dust occasionally fell to the drink below, swishing, undrinkable. Sparrows, pigeons, gulls, seagulls, whatever they were, shat, so the bridge was covered gloriously in shit. I climbed underneath. There was a platform there. Restrooms. The walls were a cage of brass tubing and titanium wires. Outside, wave lapped wave, spuming oceanward.

This was a forbidden place. I thought of robbing a vending machine. Someone else had gotten to it already. The restrooms (already mentioned) were sumptuously, unbelievably dirty. Cracks wound in the tiles. Layers of grease on the walls. Turning on the sink, no water came. Quite expectedly, this place was not conductive to the flow.

"I would expect," said a stranger, "that you aren't looking to meet strangers here."

"No," I said. "Not really."

"If you met me somewhere else," said the stranger, "would you still not want to meet me?" He had white stains in his hair, and he wore a yellow jumpsuit (ragged), and tall latex boots (seamless). Tinted glasses kept the sun away, but there was no sun here. He carried an acoustic guitar, strung, in one hand, without a case. Big hair gave him balance, a poofy element of the bereaved. At any moment it seemed he might break into song. I wondered if he could dance.

"I don't know," I said. "You don't look like you belong anywhere, so I guess you couldn't belong anywhere but here." Above, pale yellow flickered twice in sequence. This place wasn't clean enough for me. Most probably my standards were too high. I'd lived too long in a better world.

"What if I was wearing a suit?"

"You'd still have your hair," I said. "It takes up lots of space."

"Absolutely!" he exclaimed. "It does! It takes up lots of space!"

"And you look like you've never brushed your teeth before," I said. "Ever."

"Right again!" (again). "I've never brushed my teeth either!"

"Does that make you abnormal?"

"*Incorrect*," he said. "It makes me an *individual*." He clapped his hands once, dirtily. "I just have to give you the details."

And he gave me the details.

"Fascinating," I said.

Even his speech was unique.

"Think you could sing a song?" I asked. "And dance? You look like you sing songs, and dance."

"Yes I do!" he exclaimed (proudly). "I do sing, and I do dance!" So he sang, and he danced, twisting one foot, playing guitar upside down. He sang horribly, and danced horribly, but I think that was what he went for, a novelty among novelties. In all things he was painfully, irrevocably unique.

::::::::::::::::::::::

Voices

Markus
and I stared together at the sea, night-buoys aloft, the coastal patrol patrolling. Waves lapped the land like hungry tongues, to go along for all time, in defiance of the times, according to the times, a wearisome singing. Beneath, sand sifted in coolness. For being dirt, for being dusty spume, it felt surprisingly clean.

"Think there's anything out there?" I asked.

Markus picked up a handful of sand, dropped it, picked it up again.

The ocean, you mean?

Yeah, the ocean.

"Then Europe, I suppose, though we already know that."

Though maybe I should have been asking if there was anything *in* the ocean, some great, hulking secret, a bloated originality of Mother Nature, in hiding. It was ignorant of me to personify the planet as a woman. In all likelihood, if the planet were a person, it would be a hermaphrodite, both mother and father, impregnating itself, to feed the trees. In all likelihood (barring the hermaphroditic), there were very few who wanted to hear that.

"Maybe I should have said "in" the ocean," I said.

"Then I would have to say water," Markus answered.

"Yeah," I said, "I bet you're right."

::::::::::::::::::::::

I'd come to climb a mountain, which would make me a mountain climber, if I relied on statements of position. Cold streams gurgled in the breeze, frothing against the sides, to carry me home. Were there trout in there? Did they feed off wholesome current, fishlike, their scaly frames, their aquiline contribution? All streams lead to the center- all streams lead to the ocean- deep and blue, deep, infinite as unending, to land, to land. Jet-steams, sea-currents, the mountain was the intersection of mediums, crustial. The horizon split like a wire.

So here, I was here and I was really here, to feed the breeze. Winter gusts tore me. God abandoned me in cold wilderness. The desert began here, the mechanical desert: apple cores, paper wads, blots of ink, a wasteland of dimension. Hot, tumbling mounds of sand, I climbed them, holding a knife between my teeth; made ascendance up spiraling stairways, grit and pebbles, destructive.

The mountain fed me the remains of old bones. Somewhere near the top I might find an altar, the zenith point. Where you left the earth, making shots to moon, the firmament embrace. A-contextual, an exit to cancel place, to exit bleeding wounds, all in a single burst of energy. Somewhere near the top the world began. The mountain fed me the remains of old bones.

::::::::::::::::::::

Markus held his skull, shaking. Sickly sweat berated him; whole vortexes of names coerced him. Despite living in a patriotic world, he was still unhappy. (Laughing.) As if (selfless) the world still had room for patriots anymore, not here in the un-person, the neighborhood brigade. The days of kin are over, the days of sign language and slaughter.

"Are you okay?"

"Maybe," he said.

"If you had a problem," I said, you could tell me, because (sometimes) I really am good a being (something) like a friend, so it's okay- if you say it is- I keep secrets, and I have very little of the kamikaze in the me, the asylum poet, the bourgeois revolutionary; that's not who I am- or not now, at least- so if you had a problem, "you could tell me."

In life, much of what is spoken goes unsaid.

::::::::::::::::::::

—I'm not sure, he said. It's just that sometimes...

—What?

—You know, those times you're doing homework (or you would be, if you weren't so busy putting it off) or you're washing clothes at three in the morning. I picked up some money yesterday, for free, so I guess I picked up a donation, and I gave it to my mom because she wanted to buy something off a cereal box. I said Mom, seriously, you don't have to do this, really, but she said Shut up Markus, I'm your mother and what do you know about wisdom, you don't. She always brings up the fact she was alive before I was. She's so cold.

—And?

—The other day I got off the bus late (I'd fallen asleep late, you know, the way I sometimes do) and on the way home some kid almost ran into me with my bike. I carried my books and dropped them once. It embarrassed me because I thought I might have been forgetting something. Quick interruptions always make me stutter.

—What else?

—I've been hearing voices.

Voices

::::::::::::::::::::::

(Markus speaks out loud
but he says very little. I don't
know how
he puts up
with all that feedback
racking.)

::::::::::::::::::::::

"What do you think they mean?" I asked. Without realizing, I'd stood. I paced the room, from side to side, returning. Ghastly pictures assailed me, old wrappers, videogames. Markus was a real hero at guitar, but very few people knew. There were curtains by the window. If there'd been a wind, it might have blown. Neighbors are a waste of time. They need to rake their own leaves; mow their own fucking grass.

"I'm not sure," he said. Of course he wasn't sure.

"Are they trying to tell you something?"

"Maybe."

"Like what?"

"That..." he trailed off, "is just something else I don't know.

::::::::::::::::::::::

Veronica held my hand.

She breathed, working hard in the city.

As if.

"I think..." she trailed off, in sequence, "I think I'm leaving today."

"Where are you going?"

Somewhere better." She sat with one hand tracing patterns on my shoulder, another holding me there. Grabbing her wrist, I thought of telling her I didn't want her to go. We could run away to the desert, to bathe in radial flame, tracking pathways through a sea of superheated dust, hot and lifeless and ours, where the water came once a month, and blossoms bloomed rapturous in tune, a blush, of embers in rebirth.

"Yeah," she said, "somewhere better."

She held my hand. I felt emasculate and possessed. Ashamed.

"Do you need any help?" I doubt the streets take kindly to letting go of beautiful women. She shook her head. I wondered. If she didn't get away either I would see her again (tomorrow, a week from now) or no one would ever see her again. If she got away everything would be exactly the same.

"I'll miss you," I said.

"You'll be the only one."

I thought of laughing, but it wasn't funny.

I never saw her again.

:::::::::::::::::::::::

I went with James to an empty lot on the outskirts of town. Someday, I realized, he really might hurt someone. I think James' goal in life was to become a statistic, the personification of the contemporary urban youth, striking out with steal bats and sticks hastily sharpened near the end. James was the spirit of the city, in touch. Someday, his time might come.

He passed me a can of spray paint, cylindrical, a concentration of message, bright colors, jagged sketchings, language. For seeming so confident, James worked curiously quick, wanting to leave. Someday, I thought, he wouldn't be confined to dank alleys. There were no police here, though he was afraid of the police. I told him to relax, but he was still too nervous.

It's no use making statements that muffle themselves. Society the crusher has already disposed of artistry. I say that but I'm a liar trying to call myself an artist. Art changes very little, and I know that too, but sometimes I'd like to pretend the internal really does reflect the external (as if!), and I'd like to pretend we don't live in a protean ghostworld of statistical semiotic shadows; representation to the imaginary people, the proletarian sea. All things rise out of the ocean: starfish, octopus, our sick, organic ancestors, they've taken the sea with them (to land, to land!) tracking pastures in the highest mountain, planting flags on distant stars. All things are infinitesimal in nature. Of them all, the artist is the very smallest.

It's okay, I said, no one hears, but he didn't believe me, he didn't believe. Maybe being an artist, as a rule, my voice can never be heard. Not even here, where there are words on the walls. James couldn't hear because, being himself, he wasn't listening.

As a rule, I'm right far too often. Though maybe it isn't an issue of context anymore, but means of expression, of verse, of scripture. If all things are of the people, then who are they to know; in accumulation, all through history, a whole world of silent voices. In the city, the internal and the external are unrelated, a schizoid duplication. Meaning, as a rule, cannot possibly exist.

Voices

```
::::::::::::::::::::::::
```

Ironically, for
    all my
           preaching,
           we didn't
say anything
worth   listening
    to

.

```
::::::::::::::::::::::::
```

If I were to interpret dreams, I'd say I was falling out of the stars, or that the stars were falling on me. Immaculate spears of dream took me in. If I could touch them, they wouldn't move. No. If I could touch them, they wouldn't be moving, not at me, not breaking in the mirror.

I guess I'd fallen asleep on the hill. The sky sank its weight on me, and fed me stars. A dark night, waking up on a mountain outside the city- if you could call it that (which you couldn't). Fireflies phased out of existence. The grass was damp, pressing against my clothes, and I was damp with it, and we were damp together, in unification, the way time changes.

I didn't believe that. Sometimes I have trouble believing in life, in the individual, or myself, as an individual that is, in relevance to others. Understanding undermines the principles of conversation. I'd been writing poems in the darkness, at loss in a big, big ocean. As if. Renouncing the idea of place hasn't been innovative for hundreds of years.

If I had a story, this might be where it began.

Voices

III

—

in

sequence

.

...
to prove the
world
was flat,
I
went
on a great
crusade.

Voices

The rain
    came first. First
silence, then the rain, a (taptap) tapping
raindrops
falling quiet in the midnight streets droplets lying
    quiet
on the pavement quietly tires passing over
to smooth out the rain iron
                our sins
    into the floorboards
of the city down so low
not even the janitor
    remembers to clean them up
    any
more.

::::::::::::::::::::

As if
    there were order to this introduction. I could say I met her there but that would
undermine the scandalous necessities of sequence. And
    yes, I realize I'm rolling myself over, as if I could really make this
    journey back in time, but I don't think the rules apply when you're alone with
gorgeous girls
    in
    the rain.

::::::::::::::::::::

I met
    her on the vestibule,
      seeing as she was there alone. I have an affinity for strange places, facing outwards onto the night. You could see the stars from there, but it wasn't a good place to write poetry, though sometimes at noon the sun slanted at strange angles across the tiling, engraving the floor in skewed
    congruencies of light, tangled in shadow.
      Up above, the moon made faces for her. The emptiness pushed further away, a pressurized dilation, bowing down around the center. Every heart beat for her, every word to say. When it was for her, the world became real poetry, to be worthy, even for a moment. Maybe
    she would greet me. A turn of the fingers, bright flicker of straining vibes. I knew she'd heard me, because she had ears, to state things blatantly, to name an attribute of *her,*
             isolate the principles of *her*
altogether, culminating a pantheon onto herself,
    otherworldly beauty
        and
        blatant rendition (changing space). If there'd
been wind, she might have taken flight. Because
              she could soar,
altogether. On the
                  vestibule,
        I met
      her
               there.

::::::::::::::::::::

"Hello," she said.
    "Hey."
    Together. Here we were, to be with each other. I've never been an acolyte of pain, but that doesn't mean I don't understand intensity. Writhing, strings of dispersion. She had nothing phallic about her, that is to say, though really, though really. She said hello, did I worry her there? Almost seeing, she took whole galaxies

Voices

and consumed them, not into herself, not worrying. If I were a saint, I'd never have come here. But I've never had much saintly about me.

Hey. To come and see. If
I weren't a mystery, would you still be here with me: the way
      I can't help but revert to teenage lyricism *(*
          oh my bleeding heart my
   skylit eyes you hurt me once you remember
                last week we were united in our love
together making
  union
  together you I me together
taking vigil of the whole goddamn fucking country
           her cold corridors her angsts
      fire and brimstone
  poetry
rendition kissing
  furiously
       in alone places
       my love) I just met you here

really that's no way to approach the unknow-able no way to keep track of slipping time. Girl you said hello to me now I can never forget you. It's not your fault you aren't keeping track of words (I'll never forget you). Really, is that any way to make introductions I can't ask myself these questions while I'm so busy looking after whole new kinds of answers the kind you don't already see in dreams.

Moon sky sun
scribe screaming
see
        me
see me
I   am.

::::::::::::::::::::::

... that's it, I see you again.
though really, of course I'd never seen her before. She'd been eyeless, faceless, armless, legless, skinless, hairless, unreal. Dreaming of European light. I could see into my own future. I met her there, in dreams. Really. I bet she knew. She knew. (armless, legless, faceless). It's

not as though she would grow a body for me, grow legs and breasts and beautiful,
    beautiful face, though she did undermine ideas
    of regularity, the cyanide kiss,
    scent and moonlight, slipping

                                                            silently,
    a night killer, to make the darkness
bleed. I'd never
    killed before, never thought of taking steps to create. Why she made me think. Could she intoxicate me, with stories, cleanliness adjacent to vampire purity? I've never been fond of the undead, their clamminess and curling fingers. She approached me.
    Or did I approach her?

                            I

    found her there in the vestibule, steps, stones,
a stage made of glass, her own
        place,
    a kind of crying, because
                    did she cry, when I found her
                                there? I asked her questions she
                    refused to answer, not dilapidating in
                                            themselves but
                                            dissipating on
    sound. It wasn't that she couldn't speak, or that she wouldn't, but we were too good at making   silent connections, the personal kind, she and her changing faces, her starry skies.
        Truly, I wish
she was there for me, but it's
                not as though I couldn't tell my own story (or would?...); the dreams nailed into me and whole families of thought denied themselves to me. I've never been a realist, despite believing in the real,
                and I've never been religious, despite believing
    in false
    Gods.

                        ::::::::::::::::::::

Voices

I thought of telling her things, but that would only feed the complication. Monsters surrounded us, if I were to make more statements of place. Our complication defined us, our lack of a center. Feed me

MORE, FEED ME

but we weren't part of that, or I don't think we were. If there were even a choice to be made, between things and other things, reclusive. Fragmentary thought abounds me. Revolution precludes self-awareness:

OUR

...our world isn't a place for fishermen anymore. The smell of gills disgusts me.

...if this weren't real, I would tell myself

to focus more on the true,

because irony

has more fangs

than an old, rabid

dog.

...All things move inevitably toward the

center

(period)

::::::::::::::::::::

"I had a dream about you," I said, "if you'd believe me, and if that doesn't creep you out." Though the more I thought about it the more I didn't believe myself, the more frightened I was. Nameless, playing games, making jokes in a smoky bar where not even the grizzled, fantastically drunk man in the far corner found himself inclined to crude humor. If there I was, truncating. I could abbreviate myself. Punctuate. I really could.

She turned. Already she'd said hello to me. Greeting. Hey. I've never seen you before. What else is there to say? "What would that make you?" (she said.) "A dreamer?" To be struck by irony, a game in itself.

"I'm not sure," I said, "but I do dream."

"Could you see the future for me?"

"I could paint a picture of the past, maybe."

Can you paint?

Maybe.

"What are you doing here?" She turned back to the window. "Or what's up, if you feel like I'm infringing on territory, or undermining law."

"Maybe I came here to find you."

(I didn't.)

"Though maybe just to chase the boredom away." I looked back for a moment, to where the air carried traces of electricity. "I wouldn't say I don't like dancing," I said, "but I wouldn't say I like it either, if that makes sense."

"It does."

"People say strange things about you," I said.

"They do." (no question)

"Should I believe them?"

"Maybe you should."

      "It seems

like wherever I go, you're there." I took a step towards her. "And it seems like wherever I've been, you've been there

        too."

She shrugged, or the night shrugged for her. Periwinkle clouds were unlit in the darkness. Cool rain berated us. The moon showered her in pools of sinuous light. I'd never seen a girl more beautiful, though it wasn't as though I had a right to judgment, not taking myself into consideration, that hollowness that was me, mind, sight, hearing, to channel the city and pass it through. I wish we could say we were alone on a balcony, but the vestibule contained me, there with too many corners, a stifling limit to space.

"If you believe the stories about me," she said, "maybe they're true."

"Are they really stories?"

"Depending on if you understand language."

      "Do

you feel like dancing?" I asked. "If it was with you,

        I would care to dance."

"Not really," she said, "or not now. I like it better in the moonlight."

Connection devoured us, if that was what you wanted to call it.

::::::::::::::::::::

My friend wanted me to go to a party. I went without caring what I wrote. Inside the lights were green blue red purple orange pink flaring. I wasn't late enough for vomit to be involved. Maybe it was a dance, which would explain why so many people were dancing. Somebody passed me a drink. Somebody threw me a gesture. Wherever I was.

Parties are not a good place to meet people. We were all strangers here.

Voices

I met her in the vest
          ibule, which implies more things than one
          (clavicle, cubicle, silvery dress the darkness
glint- none of those things) for whatever reason I did. But now I'm just repeating
myself. Fuck time and place.
    When it was with her, you didn't need them anymore.

::::::::::::::::::::

"Do you want to dance?" I asked.
    "Yeah," she said, "yeah, I think I do, but I don't think I want to leave."

                We danced-
       if that was what you wanted to call it. Turbulent winds
           encircled us, and sense of shrouding,
    not necessarily that which is known. To spin, we spun on axis. Her dress (she
                was
wearing a dress) bared her shoulders to me, her slimness, a sense
             of litheness and ebony clouds.
The rain
was pounding, a song kept playing and though we couldn't feel it the wind kept
blowing. Omnipotence embraced us, we were everywhere
and we were really there.
    She was a beam of light capturing the moon, she was
    a vicious intensity of sensation.
I danced with her in the moonlight.
    With every breath
    she was
    beautiful.

        Are you here alone? I asked.
        Promise me
you won't tell me your name.
        I promise.
        That's not enough sometimes, just to promise.
        It's okay, I've
        forgotten

already. I've forgotten
for you, just
to show
I care, in case you didn't believe.
Are you here
alone?

"Maybe I am," she said. "No, no I don't think so."
"Is it me?" I asked. "You don't want me here?"
"No," she said, "if you want, you can stay."
Hello *(if*
you greet me that
way, coming
from your lips,
it makes
me never
want
to
leave)
She smiled, and she embraced me.
I felt, by sorcery, we might
placate new murder, waving forward
and onto
(a thunder)
embrace
,
and I stayed.

If we'd been outside, we never
would have left the
r
a
i
n.

Voices

I
haven't broken pages in quite a while. I guess that would make me inconsistent. I'm more things than one, and in being so many, I cancel myself. Sometimes
I wonder if I trust *myself* to be consistent, the less in touch I get with myself, the more I fall out   of a cycle of days (nights nights). That makes me wonder where I'm going, where I've been. There are
so many people in here it's like I'm at war with a very large number of very evenly matched opponents. While in being so many, we cease to be at all.

::::::::::::::::::::::

I've been hearing voices.

::::::::::::::::::::::

James didn't look so good. Sweat (the real kind, streaked with dirt) made rivers down him, a plastered glove. His shirt was torn. His eyes were fear. I'd never seen James fear before, especially not here in his element, where everyone knew him, where we were all together. There was a limp in his step. I bet he'd fallen.

"What's up?" I asked, because there wasn't much else I could say, not with him looking like this. But was it different this time, could I say? James knelt against the wall, as though the atmosphere wouldn't put up with him anymore: sputtering incoherence, the scared kind, the grievous. Maybe, just maybe, he meant it to be language.

"Shit," he said, "they're after me." (Without indication, without a basis in crime.) I asked who. This time I didn't know. James knew when not to be liberal. He knew these streets like an old, dry bone.

"I'm not sure," he said, "but they're scary, and they're big."

"Are they still coming?"

"I'm not sure," he said. "Maybe I lost them. I knew I'd find you here." He glanced back to my mural, my grand great escape, plastered to the wall above, beside, my little unnatural world. No one had seen it. I'd never been here before either. I have no idea how he found me.

"Can you help?" he asked.

"I can do my best," I said. "Is there anywhere safe?"

"Not here."

"Then maybe they can find this. Should I write them a message?"

"Do you think they'd understand?"

"No... no I don't think so."

"Then let's just go."

::::::::::::::::::::::

I looked at myself in the mirror. I wasn't there, but it was something like I was. I saw myself, I believed. He had my face, my arms, my legs. He moved when I moved, looking back at me. But sometimes I couldn't keep track, thinking that was me, in reflection, seeing myself in the immaterial, falling into circles of misrepresentation.

It made me feel like less than myself, like many. It was frightening.

The heavens
fed me darkness, but the water was smooth. All off and into the distance, it was smooth, only rippling where I moved. Way in the distance, the bottom
lit up, a gentle glowing, above the water. The stars, glinting and reflecting, were there with me, and my world was a reflection of the sky,
little bulbs of whiteness, waving in the mirror.
Maybe, if I kept walking, I could go somewhere. Footfalls on unmoving waves. Down below there might have been a current.

::::::::::::::::::::::

Voices

They came for us on the streets. They were scary. James saw them, fearing. They made it difficult to run, but did I fear them? They were negative vibes and testosterone danger, but did I fear them? We ran. I'm not sure why he wanted my help when all we could do was run.

Monsters followed us.

Or not exactly monsters, but I couldn't bring myself to describe them. They were bigger than us, and they wore skin, but they didn't smell right, and they only had one eye. James, a few steps ahead, pushed an old lady out of the way, running through an intersection. I followed. Chaotic streams en-circled us. I almost fell, and I barely managed to get through alive. James turned into an alley and almost broke his ankle in the process.

When I saw them I understood (immediately). James had bad karma (the worst). He'd referred to them in plural. I equalized. I've never been fond of taking burdens, but I suppose it must have been unavoidable. I'm good at being (something) like a friend.

"You know," I said, "they're never going to stop chasing you. They're slower than us, but they're stronger, and they don't have to think like the city. They can break through walls."

"It doesn't matter."

"Dude, I'm sorry, I don't think I believe you."

"It's okay," he said, "just run with me for a while. We'll think of something."

"Do you have a hydrogen bomb?"

"If I did, it probably wouldn't do us any good."

::::::::::::::::::::

Of course, they didn't have any problem
getting through the intersection.
They could go through cars
just as easy as walls.

::::::::::::::::::::

We stopped, breathing hard, and came to rest in another part of the city. It was gray down here, and old. There were ghosts here (the real kind) and they were real too, almost enough that you could touch them. Withered, musty, they sat weakly in twos, in threes, to sing forgotten songs and play joyless old games. I couldn't tell if they'd always been there, or if they were just making appearances for our sake.

James leaned against the wall, vivaciously alive like me. We were antigens here, in the freezer. Jealousy spun
like a swarm of spiders.

"Are we safe?"

"For a while," he said. "No one comes down here."

"Ever?"

"The light hasn't shone here for almost a hundred years." He straightened up.

"They can't get us yet. Not for a while."

I squinted. Shadow filigreed the corridor.

I had no idea where we were, or how we'd gotten here. First I thought we'd gone under a bridge; then I thought we'd hidden in an abandoned factory; then I thought we'd holed out in the subway. We obviously hadn't done any of these things. Wherever we were, it was something like a corridor, tapering (tapering?) at the ends. Looking back, there might have been light, but maybe there wasn't. It felt like we'd gone underground. The heaviness of the city fell on us, flattening the balance.

On either side we saw old women knitting scraps of cloth (filmed with dirt, with grease), many times sown over. I said the men sang songs, but they sang silently, in the past, so no notes came, except for maybe an echo down the hall. There were no children here. They were silent, shivering people, papery thin, as strung onto an alpha death, a personalized fissure in continuity.

"What are we going to do?" I asked. "We can't stay here long."

"No," he said. "I don't think we can." Looking up. They were beginning to notice us. Yellow eyes rolled in hallow sockets, slowly, shallowly, a laxness of motion. The walls echoed, an undercurrent of mumbling. They came to life slowly, like an old, dry gas. They were the bottled fart of the city. Wool rustled wool, whispering in the corridor. It wasn't safe here anymore. In just a few moments we would have to leave.

"Come on," James said. A few were even standing now, looking in our direction. They moaned for us, wishing strength to fingers, fortitude to bones. We taunted with youth. We discarded their memory. It wasn't what we'd come to do, but we were tomb raiders stumbled accidentally onto forgetfulness. When they reached for us, we pulled away, and when they called to us, we pretended not to hear.

This was an easy place to lose yourself, drowning in silent voices.

::::::::::::::::::::::

Voices

I led Markus across a boundless plane of water, shimmering like aquiline glass. Our steps made ripples, but we didn't fall. Way up high, the sky was a shadow caught in blackness, with little specks showing through. We had a long way to go.

"Don't fall," I said. "Just make sure you don't fall. Because then you'll be falling, and it's a long way down." Into whatever secret the darkness keeps, at the very bottom, pressurized coldness, hidden in the water. I didn't know why we were here- couldn't know- why I'd come, why I'd been given a sense of self and the horizon. But I led. I led because (sometimes) I could be something like a leader.

Markus stumbled.

"Jesus," he said.

And a minute later: "I don't know how much further I can go."

"Just keep going," I said, and took a step, leaving my own tracks in the dampness. "And don't fall. Please, whatever you do, just don't fall."

::::::::::::::::::::

"What did you do?" I asked.

James took a breath. He was sweating still, heavily. Together we were a tired, aching duplex of sweat, of pain. His karma was coming for us. His karma was a one eyed monster, two of them. It moved slow, but it would get us in the end. Karma was phallic, and it jabbed profusely. Karma smelled like lemon juice and rotten eggs, like slime and unshaven armpits. No matter how hard I tried, I couldn't stop breathing.

"You were there," James said.

"I was?"

"When I crossed the line."

"Shit." I massaged a hurting thigh. "I told you not to. No one ever takes my advice." James laughed. He was still sweating. "They're going to get you," I said, "you know. We can run, but karma doesn't sleep like a person, it doesn't hurt or eat." And as an afterthought: "They can go through walls."

"Yeah," he said. "I know."

"Then why'd you want me to come with you?"

"Because you'll remember," he said. "Is your camera on?"

"Yeah," I said. "It's always on, you know that."

"Then you'll remember," he said, "because you're good with memory."

::::::::::::::::::::

James was wrong, of course.
I've never trusted memory. That's why I had the camera
in the first place.

::::::::::::::::::::

I looked into the mirror, in tiredness. It was strange. I fogged myself over, the color of skin, hair and eyes and whiteness. Maybe I'd been sleeping wrong, if I slept, eyes, together, falling out of synchrony, falling, that doubling up in the picture, that splitting vision. I rubbed my eyes, if I had them. It did nothing for tiredness. There I was, the ghost of an image, extravaganza of voices, built (carefully) out of pure lies, a great fucking *temple* of lies, bound together, and tearing.

If vision blurred, it did so on its own, no part of me, inside, my sense of self, my world of being. Colors had long since fled from the world. I had taken them into myself, to recreate, to persevere. No, but where the instantaneous existed in duplication, where I went the image split. *I went on a journey over*
a cold ocean, and
the darkness fed me
stars.

::::::::::::::::::::

We spun around by a gas station, still running. Fat bearded men stood pumping fuel. Two lamps shone, though it hadn't gotten dark yet. There were cars, trucks, and hermaphroditic, androgynous hybrids of the two, end over end, palpating replenishment. The woman behind the counter looked very bored, and made her boredom clear, scanning stamps, smoking. James ran into more than a few people. I didn't remember ever being so tired, so challenged by breathing.

James opened a door.

"Get in," he said. "Jesus, hurry up."

"Dude no," though I thought of going, I really did. "We are *not* going to steal a car." Speaking hurt. "That's what got us here in the first place. Sort of."

He beckoned, still sweating. Disappointment etched him, sadness and fear. "Are you sure?" he asked. I said I was. "We're making a horrible mistake."

"I don't care," I said, though I didn't understand what I was saying.

He shut the door, bitterly. "I can't believe you."

"We have to go," I said. "They're still coming."

"Yeah," he said. "Let's go."

Voices

And they were coming:

stirring up dust and knocking aside cars, all brutal and ugly, with their raging, unnatural faces, their phallic gazing. Loose skin hung over thick bones. It swung as they ran, garroted on mongoloid torsos, the hideous thickness of thighs and spine. They growled loudly, and deeply, but without breathing. No words left them, no sounds of company. They saw nothing, felt nothing. Roaring, long and loud, deeply.

They came.

We ran for the inside of the store. Hopefully there was a door. It wouldn't do to hide in bathrooms because they could pass through walls. And there I go again, repeating myself. The woman gave us bored looks, scanning stamps, smoking. We knocked over customers, afraid. We were not good for business. The shelves almost fell for of us, and we were frantic spillers of coffee.

In our wake, we brought demons. They knocked over the shelves we hadn't gotten to, and spilled even *larger* amounts of coffee, breaking records, burning. They had two eyes together, unblinking. Slushies were unfit for them, as were candy, chips, cola. They feasted on fear, but they ran slowly.

Luckily for us, there was a back door.

::::::::::::::::::::

James hurt himself. And we were moving, so he hurt himself painfully. He tripped, and he was rolling, and he almost sprained his ankles. One knee bled. His lips and gums bled too. I helped him up. We looked back for a moment. Way in the distance, they were still coming. With the rumble of buildings, making cracks in the sidewalk.

"Can you keep going?"

"Yeah," he said, "but this would be so much easier if we'd just stolen that car."

James committed his crimes on a grand scale. I knew I'd be fine, because no one notices artists, even when you paint pictures on walls, but James was a focal point of the regular, a fanatic visage of the now. The derelict face of the city, he was steel and concrete, deep, deep corridors, paved over memory. Karma had two eyes for him, and vengeance.

And I had a vision of possibility.

He drove,

but he couldn't go far because he couldn't leave the city. There was no place for him in this world, but he could fade away, making desperate grasps at departure. Neither of us had control of position, or any hand to maneuver context, just we were opposite ends, context and character, realization and being. He was a part of this place, its soul and body, messenger of the streets. The city was no-person. He in return. It didn't care if he wanted to leave. He was the place, in definition, in act and execution. With all my heart, I pitied him. If not, I wouldn't have run for him. When he was gone, he would leave a hole.

The desert was quiet at night. He drove. Cacti, statuesque in the shadows, were pale and unthreat-ening. Tumbleweeds tumbled, flipping in the sand. A thin moon knifed the horizon. James smoked. He knew this would be his last cigarette. When his time came, he would go with it, given options, to fade, or make faded.

"If you want," he said, "I could drop you off at the edge of the city, so you didn't have to walk as far."

"No, it's okay," I said, "I'll walk. I've never been in the desert at night before."

"Whatever you want." And he kept driving.

I got out ten minutes later, waving as he left.

The next day, they would find his car, empty, off the side of the road.

I hadn't realized, of course, when he asked, that I was making the choice for him. How he was going to go: by his own will, by others; final journeys onto darkness, that subliminal, pivotal decay. The light passed through. He shimmered like dust. The dawn would not bring rain. I hadn't realized, until he bled, that I'd become his arbiter of change, his judgment of decease. It was because of me he ran. I owed it to him to keep running.

So we ran.

A hundred feet behind, they followed. They saw (only us, thought, felt) only us. We were their means of destination, their subject in matter. Smaller than they were, more human than they were: the mighty hand, downblow of crushing force, compression. They followed with one eye, seeing only, one, individual purpose, acclimation and death. It isn't possible to explain how badly they scared me.

::::::::::::::::::::

Markus fell
with a stumble,
all in and down, to become the water. He'd been complaining for miles now of tiredness and decay, a weakness in the bones, but I thought he could go on,
I really did.
The sky was quiet, and no wind blew, here in the
decease. An orange glow bubbled, hazing in the softness. No fish swam. A silvery glint overtook sharp edges.
Markus
broke the surface with a rush, descending.

Voices

He was a night-diver hurled onto secret depths, overwhelmingly small, and
      liquid clouds reached out to him, blanketing in ginger fields, golden sun, an
auburn flare, expunging heart and mind, to fade, to fade. Swirls masked him, and
more colors now: flaming gold, garnet fire, spears of purple, altogether an
                    omniscient, ominous
      swallowing, reaching to engulf him in warmth. I watched until he fell out of
sight, and long after, remembering his tiredness, too early to diagnose
        weakness, too early to contemplate grief, a quagmire of dimension.
      No fish swam. The stars would not

   f

    a

   l

    l

   for me.

::::::::::::::::::::::

"This way!" James turned down an alley, past gravel strewn disgustingly, markings
of pain. Sick trash laid careless, the defecation of a generation: gum-wrappers,
paper cups, rusting pins. Arrows, chalked to the walls beside, pointed in opposite
directions, misleading. The air grew thick with dirty mist.

I grabbed his arm. He turned, rasping. "We can't go this way," I said. "There's no
way out, there's no way..." Inside I made recreations, not remembering, and
condemned us for fear, insidious certainty. I knew this place, this alley. We weren't
welcome here, by the spiders, the rats and oil; struck then by images of ailing
growth, organic, fermenting skin, dappling parameters... what, by that smell, one
gross, rotting carcass. I'd been here before. I knew the smell of death.

"What?" he said, "why?" but he knew, he must have known, because he knew
this city, its every turn, its every bend and corridor. The maze had been made clear
to him, to be manipulated. Manipulate it he did. He took shortcuts, he ran through
hidden places. To him no place was hidden, no place too secret. Back here where it
smelled like shit, where the spiders were.

"There's no way out," I said. "We can't get away."

"I know."

"Why did you bring us here?"

Though of course I knew.

They blocked out the alley- around the corner now, into sight. Unlike them, we
couldn't go through walls. Unlike them, only one of us would leave. Standing

motionless, they waited patiently, one eye ahead. Only the young die proud. Try as he might, he had never been young, he had never been.

He turned to shake my hand.

"It was nice running with you," he said.

Weird.

It was.

He took a step but

turned back.

"Oh yeah," he said, "I heard he's ready to meet you."

"Who?"

"You'll know," he said. "When the Chimera wants to meet you, you always know." He laughed, and he'd given up sweating. Sometimes, I wish I had the option.

"I guess I'll see you later," I said.

"You won't," he said, as he left.

And, of course, I didn't.

Voices

I played
basketball with Travis again, for whatever reason. Sometimes I wish he'd just give up, but he never does. At least it makes me feel like a friend, for being gentle. I did a good job keeping secrets, even his own. He took baths in delusion. He'd seen so many commercials they were starting to rot away at his brain.

There we were,
in the beating sun. Ten minutes ago it hadn't beat. It must have changed frequencies, making acclimation to the game. I hate basketball. Every time I dribble it wounds me. I think Travis

knew this. I wondered if he did.

"Someday," he said, "I'll beat you."

He said this every day, but he seemed to believe.

And sometimes, I almost believed him too.

It's
not as though I had any right to cut him down, any permission to justify statistics. Though of course, he wasn't exactly on a role. Maybe someday he really would. But I doubted it.

Travis stretched.

"Someday," he said, "I'll really beat you." Having gotten into a habit of repeating himself.

The sky was blue. The sun beat down.

"Hey dude." I looked to the sky, the beating sun.

"Yeah?"

"I'm not sure if you knew, but if I was a good friend, I would tell you Jacob was fucking your sister."

"Yeah," he said, "I know."

"You do?"

"Of course I do." He dribbled. "Whenever Jacob comes over, he disappears for fifteen minutes. Saying he has to take a piss, though course he *doesn't* have to take a piss. And sometimes he disappears for fifteen more."

Oh. "I was just making sure."

"My sister's a whore," he said.

"You probably shouldn't generalize like that," I said. I wish he wouldn't subjugate so carelessly. On some level, I felt mildly offended.

"My sister's a whore," he repeated, "and I know that too."

He dribbled. The goddamn shitting pissing sun showering flame. The shitting pissing showering sun. The sky was blue. Travis dribbled, taking the word, bending its context by virtue of repetition.

"People think I don't know," he said, "but I know." He dribbled. "I comprehend. Just sometimes it's better to pretend you don't. Sometimes pretending is so easy it's almost beautiful."

The sun beat down.

I understood.

::::::::::::::::::::

They came to me in the process of creation. There
were
two of them, one large, one small: messengers of some grander being, acolytes of the furious sun. They stood, silent, until I noticed them, though I'd noticed them already. I imagined they wore suits (the expensive kind), and wide, reflective sunglasses. In their own way, they looked some sort of cosmic secret agents. I suppose, in their own way, they probably were.

"Is he ready for me?" I asked. They nodded.

I left with them, and they led me through whole different realms of the city, past old pawnshops with crooked dealers, closed down
buildings, abandoned warehouses, derelict suburbs... and then back, onto a high, industrious street I'd never seen before, where the buildings were taller than the sky, and they glinted in the afternoon, a whole rainbow of city-color, in height... down a great flight of stairs, under archways, to a specialized, rarified void. In all things, it was absolutely, astoundingly authentic.

They told me to wait, without telling. When the Chimera was ready for me, I would know. There were other people here, in
raucous conversation,

but they didn't seem to notice me, not sparing a glance, not seeing. Azure light sprinkled through glorious openings in the ceiling. But despite everything, the place had a touch of shabbiness about it, at odds in the real.

I tried to start conversation with statues. They ignored me. And I realized, a moment too late, that they weren't people at all, they didn't even *move*, not when you looked closely, and they didn't talk either, it's just

they felt like they did, two together, three, standing alone. They were an astounding kind of golem, all wreathed in magic. But I bet, sometimes, when someone came the Chimera *didn't* want to see, they weren't so intent on staying quiet. They were an excellent form of torture. A few, most likely, would

grow

fangs.

:::::::::::::::::::::

I made passage across a
gigantic, shimmering ocean, for myself, for others.

No, I traveled alone; I'd always known that, no matter

how hard I pushed for resiliency. A turquoise

mist rose from the surface. No matter what, I swore I wouldn't fall, not giving into the mirror, not breaking cleanly in two. But it was harder now, than ever before.

It didn't matter if I'd always been alone, if I was really going anywhere. I was here and I was really here, and there was no choice but just to

keep going.

I looked into the mirror. My image sprang up, a dualistic **shadow**, riding separate waves of light. I gave off my own shade, indescribable. The sky, growing to ease, was gentler now, like a real sky. And there I was, me, in the water.

Thrice above, *below,* entangled. I'd been wearing my clothes for a bit too long, and, ironically, very little of me had come into contact with the surface. I thought of posing for myself, to strike a grandiose figure, but it didn't matter, I was already there. The water was a magnificent reversal:

as above, magnified
below.

:::::::::::::::::::::

"You know," I said, "I don't really feel like playing." I passed him the ball. The sun beat down. Grass folded in the heat, sweating chlorophyll, turning brown. "We have poignant conversation sometimes, you know." I turned around. "Let's just do something else."

"Just one more game," he said.

"I think I'm going to pass out." And to make something clear: "You're insane." Still standing there so

insanely

enthusiastic, grinning, as though he hadn't just lost, as though there were somewhere great to go from here. Birds flew by. Ants crawled deep underground, carrying mold in pieces to their fat, fattening queen, to make her bigger, to churn out a greasy crop of

themselves, soulless, in multiplication; so she could

spit them out, so there could be more, and better bread. I crossed my fingers, and wished we'd thought to bring something to drink, so I could drown Travis in it. We had poignant conversation sometimes, we really did, though obviously, this

wasn't one

of them.

He passed me the ball. "Here, it's yours first."

"I don't think it matters," I said, "I'll still beat you."

"Someday," he said, "that'll change."

::::::::::::::::::::

They opened the door for me. White poured from the sanctuary beyond, cleaving a line on the floorboards, lighting fires on the wall. I stepped through, hesitating. The doors shut, too loud, not loud enough.

Strangely, the Chimera looked about like I thought he would.

We were the same height, with brown hair. He was slim, looking just a little too small for his clothes, jeans trailing on the floor, hands in pockets. Curling mist clung to him. Odd patterns, reflected from other parts of the room, hit him in every direction. He had more than one shadow, no, he had an infinite number of shadows- larger, smaller, some of them moving, leaving and walking away. When he raised an arm, molecules wavered, and, unless he didn't want them to, glasses fell off shelves, mirrors broke. In his own way, he was the extrovert center of the universe, taking action in the chaos. Despite the acne, he had a very handsome smile.

"I like the statues," I said. "And your place."

Wherever it is.

Voices

Simultaneously, I felt like I was in an attic, an alleyway, an entrance hall, and a whole number of nameless, overlapping places. There were no details. A chair became a table, became a lamppost, became a very large TV. Myriad bursts of energy, curtailing, turned the room to a cesspool of the baroque, in itself, with the complexity of good music. Despite everything, it was startlingly familiar.

"The gargoyles can be dangerous," he said. "If you aren't careful, or if you bug them too much. Some of them

grow

fangs."

"I think they scared me." I said.

"They can do that."

Electricity cackled as he blinked an eye. Whole dimensions grew thin. For some reason he was slightly less intimidating then I figured he'd be. It definitely wasn't the blue lighting that flashed in my mind, or the crazy, crazy vibrations, all in and down, playing games with rules, possibly suspending gravity. A few feet to my right, a teacup, floating in the air, became a small animal. He had the power to create life. He had the head of a lion, the tail of a snake, and the body of goat. With every breath, he unleashed an outpour of fire. I'm not sure why he didn't scare me.

"Just so you know," he said, "I owe you a favor. For running with James."

"You knew him?"

"I knew *of* him," he said, "though that doesn't really matter, as so did everything else."

"But why didn't you help him yourself?"

"I didn't owe him a favor."

::::::::::::::::::::::

"Did I ever tell you," Travis asked, "about the first time I experienced the game? And why I like it. "

I asked if he meant the first time he watched it, but

"No, it wasn't like that, I didn't watch anything." He dribbled. "It was spiritual. It was pure deepness and immersion. The game," (I'd always thought it was funny how he called it that, all dignified, as though it possessed some vilified significance, which, to him, it probably did) "it has its own life, it's own ebb and flow. Every moment is glory, every flicker in movement, bead of sweat, turn of the eyes. And when the crowd cheers, they really cheer, because you're living for them, playing the game. When you're on the court, you can be their unquestionable God, their anchor to praise, and they'll raise their hands for you, and love you, and lift you up, until you aren't human anymore, you're at the absolute center of everything that is (heart, mind, sacrifice). Basketball is the only way in the world to escape anonymity, to stop being just a person and become *you*. It makes you matter. It makes you real. None of us understand what it means to be real- not like you would understand what I mean, being an artist. The game makes us real, in its perfect, perfect embrace, lifted up, in the very center, when we make the perfect jump. It's a flash of cameras, a parade onto living rooms, corner streets, doctors' offices. Everyone screams, lifting furious voices, the announcers, the fans. I heard it from the other room. I'd been playing videogames, but what were videogames to this? Absolute proudness, a latex rhythm, sole swiping sole... he'd made a shot from half court, you understand, from *half* court, and they stood for him, they clapped for him, they cheered for him. And I came out, and I watched. It was over so fast. And then I watched again the next day, and the next. There's nothing like the thrill of renewal, of another game. Basketball is our only form of infinitude, in repetition. Every year it comes again, season upon season, each expansive in themselves, branching out like causeways in dimension, spangled fingers in the social pathos. Basketball is a microchasm of society; in size, all function. It epitomizes humanity, in all we are. Our need to compete, our need to make better. It chronicles history, moving backwards, past emperors and sultans, new rules, the current generation, and like history it has its heroes, its points of diversion. And maybe you don't understand," Travis went on, because apparently he was good at that, going on, "but basketball is everything in the world, altogether. And it doesn't matter that I'm not any good- because I know that, I comprehend, I really do, even though everyone makes fun of me when I lose. But it doesn't matter, I'm touching something better, something perfect, and, through that, it makes me perfect, and I feel like I matter. And it doesn't matter if I really do, or if other people understand, because *fuck* other people. They don't understand basketball, and because of that, they don't understand life, or self-awareness, or whatever you want to call this, here and now, in the time and place, reaching out with body and mind, spirit and fortitude, to overcome everything in this concrete crashing, this temple of cacophonous quiet, all wrapped up in a multitude of layering voices, blending until they're nothing but a stagnant, staggering silence, canceling itself, and crawling, pitifully, all through the narrowing tunnel that is time, as though it were really taking us somewhere, to some vortex way in outer space, where heaven is, if we can even really talk about such a place. Heaven doesn't exist, not on a human level, and you know that too, even better than I do." He looked at me, and he shook his fist, and he was a ridiculous fire of overflowing passion, red bands crawling in his face, flushing him different colors, making him bloat. "This world is a goddamn map of telephone poles, a flat, papery town, like in the old movies, where no one's noticed yet that the walls are falling down. We need something to hold onto, a beacon rising in the sky, luminous in bright colors, painted orange and black, so the world can see; a monument for all that is human in the anonymous age; a marker leading us to transcendence, or deliverance, or whatever you want to call it. Basketball is the skeleton key to identity, the latex doorway to the very deepest recesses of the soul."

::::::::::::::::::::::

"Do you mind if I tell you a story?" the Chimera asked.

I said it was fine.

It was strange to hear the Chimera asking questions.

"When I was young, just a few years old, I had a dream." Casually, he flicked a finger, and from it came a cackle of energy. "I still remember it, barely. It was about a wall, and steps, and climbing into the light." He paused for a moment, examining himself, in relevance to everything else. Dwarfing it.

"I woke up (in the dream) at the bottom of a huge wall. There were huge blocks in it, going way up. It was so bright I could barely see. I tried to stand, but gravity held me down. I ran my hands alone the wall. It was smooth, though it looked rough. There were no shadows in the block, only one color in the grain. I tried to stand again, pushing at the wall, but it didn't matter, I couldn't. But I looked up, and there was the light, pouring over. So instead of standing I crawled, for as long as I could, and the grass made razorblades on my arms, cutting in, and the air pressed down so hard I could barely breathe.

"After that," he raised both wrists and touched held them together, "I crawled until both of my arms bled, until both of them were soaked in blood, until I couldn't crawl any more. But the wall was still there, and it was even stronger than before, just as tall. I reached out and touched it again, lovingly, and I laid there looking up, over the wall, in a pool of spreading redness. Behind, for maybe fifty feet, I'd left a thickening trail, getting wetter. No flowers grew. I wanted to see an orchid, or a carnation, or a lilac, but there were no flowers, just the wall. And then I stood.

"It was impossible, but somehow I managed stand, and I kept going. The whole way, I leaned on the wall, because it was stronger than me, more real. I didn't walk so much as I staggered, like an old man, dying one step at a time. And then up ahead I saw a staircase, coming from the wall. The steps were big, and tall, and wide, and I couldn't walk anymore, but I took them, crawling arm over arm. Quite a few times I hit my face on the rock. Just as many I almost fell. The higher I went, the heavier it got. Cosmos pasted matter to groveling in the sand. But I kept crawling until I got to the edge."

"What was there?"

"Nothing," he said, "just a boundless sea of white, an infinite, flowing ocean. But I kept crawling, and then I fell, like heavy, heavy rock, into a void where it wasn't *possible* to fall anymore, and direction didn't matter."

"What happened then?" I asked.

"I woke up."

"Oh."

"And when I opened my eyes, everything in my room (the bed, the lamp, me), was

        f

      l

         o

          a

           t

            i

             n

              g."

"Did anything happen after that?"

"It never

came   down.

"

"Oh," I said. "Did it really happen?"

"The dream?"

"Yeah."

"Maybe." He laughed. "I've never told anyone before, just so you know."

"Then why did you tell me?"

"Because I've heard... that you're good with memory." He paused. "Is your camera on?" For some reason I was surprised. I'd assumed he knew. "I was hoping," he said, "that your camera would be on."

"Yeah," I said. "It's on."

                    :::::::::::::::::::::

Voices

The sky was blue. The sun beat down.

A car drove by. Ripples coagulated, an optical swelling. Travis dribbled. He wore a jersey, numbered, and shorts, colored. Sweat escaped him, the unattractive kind. It matted clothes to him. Disgustingly. My skin burned. Rust grew over mountains of metal. The dust was not refreshing. But there were worse places to be than here.

"I don't know if I ever told you before," I said, "but you know that Jacob kid, the one we hang out with sometimes, who's fucking your sister? I don't think I like him very much."

Travis missed another shot. Apparently, it shot a surge of elation through him. He grinned. This was his ultimate fulfillment, his anchor in the dark.

"No," he said. "I don't think I like him much either. But no one does, so it's okay."

We played. He missed another shot. He dribbled. The sun beat down. As we played, my mind wandered. Travis and I did have poignant conversations sometimes, but not very often. I stole the ball, but I missed. I wanted to write a poem about redundancy. Travis got the ball.

He scored.

The net *whooshed* all strange like, whipping as the shot passed through, and the ball bounced off the side of the court.

We paused.

"Jesus," I said.

"Jesus." He scratched his scalp, confused.

We stood, dumbfounded, as the wind picked up. Scraps of leaves scrambled in gusts. Clouds, pulsing away, turned dark, ominous colors, and the sky cleared, in all directions, moving away from the axis of *us,*

pulsing back

because we'd torn something free, that was, that wasn't supposed to be. The sky turned gray. The sun hid in shadows. Delirious, a rhythmic affront to continuity- diamonds- all- gleaming- for some abrupt disintegration, to make clear the consequences of an end, here and now, in a bastardized place, undone, by some pernicious fluctuation in the rules, breaking.

A few feet past the post, by the ball,

a green globule grew out of the ball, ionic

with emerald lightning in the side, as it took the strenuous into itself,

enlarging strangely, all but flickers in the coming dark. Static flashes,

faster than eyes, sprang out, lighting pieces of grass

on fire, wickedly, so they curled, in

Kyle Muntz

a fit
of ruination,
all things   casting aside   the
real.
Reality gave a vicious,
curdling scream, and split in twine
as it
kept growing,
a conical beam in the center, vibrating,
all the
things inside
as they grew. . .
Reality split
and the ball
went nuclear,   sending
a spear

of brightness
into the center of the storm,
where the thunder was,
the angry clouds,
swirling,
into a tornado,

spreading out

like a tear
in the

universe.

::::::::::::::::::::

I fell.

Which is to say I broke the water, splashing, hands and feet, scrabbling once, with a grasp I didn't have. The surface rebuked me, in failure, and I fell. Deeper and deeper, but slowly, waves, cloudlike in the undertow,

Voices

enfolded me,

so cool, so *neutral*, that the water might not have
been water at all, lacking wetness, and liquid fortitude. I breathed, but of course I
breathed, going under in the darkness, reaching out, opine, for a handhold

in

the light.

But

the light

was done with me, because I wasn't strong enough
to take my own advice. I was naked

here, in the sinking place, nimble, wearing a glove
of a body, just a hint of skin. Way out, casually swimming figures, invisible from
above, swam with me. They were impassive, but of course they were impassive. This
was their   place here.

It was

all they knew. Kaleidoscopic colors, welling cumulus from below, cushioned
descent, a fall onto opium dreams and lazy, lazy swaying. Already

I

knew nothing of memory, that bane, and the confines of

me,

the gap in the universe that was

me,

in line with itself, as though there were really anything
loose, in silence. Layers

peeled away

as I fell, as simplicity came true, casting aside the actual, the
factual, the

unnecessary.

Who was I, who in moments

such as these

thought nothing

of being understood?

I fell

into the darkness

and nothingness

cared for me there.

::::::::::::::::::::::

"Thanks a lot for seeing me," I said.

The Chimera nodded.

"People say that a lot," he said.

And most likely, they did.

"Just one question," I said. "Have you ever thought... maybe that you were still falling?"

"No one ever stops falling," he said. "All life is nothing but just a really, really long fall."

"Then I'll remember for you," I said, "If I can, though really, I'm not very good with memory, like people say, and I'm not very good with secrets either.

A whirlwind sprang up beside me. Pathways sprang up.

I felt like I'd been here before. I felt like I'd seen him before. This place was nothing but strangeness.

"Thanks for the favor," I said. "Maybe someday I'll need it."

"You will."

"I will?"

Why?

"I don't know if you'll believe this," he said, "but she wasn't alone."

"If you want," I said, "I could get her to talk to you. Maybe."

Markus shook his head, but he was smiling inside. He slapped himself in the face. He gurgled, strangely, and choked on inhalation, thinking of her. This was his gracious, goodliness of romance, his beacon of want, and lust, and fear. I knew, of course, that most likely she would reject him (had in fact rejected him already, so many times, by being there, by being), but there are times in life (like this) that I do my best to be (something) like a friend.

"No," he said, "you couldn't... no." But inside he was saying yes, because she was his voracious angel, and he wanted her, from a distance.

"Are you sure?"

No he wasn't. Of course he wasn't sure. He felt like he was impeding on the distance he knew. I felt for him. I wonder if he understood how far away she really was, a guest in her own self. Ashley, subliminal, was a piece of plastic with fresh, heavy breasts and extremely inviting skin. She'd told me so in person. I was willing to lie for her.

::::::::::::::::::::::

Very painfully

she rejected him, stabbing with blades of apathy, atop an undertone of disgust. He wouldn't talk about it (I don't think I wanted him to), but he told me he didn't think he would ever be able to look at her again, in this life. She was his licentious vat of acid. She destroyed him.

"Sometimes," I said to her, "you aren't very nice."

"No one ever said I had to be."

"If I could," I said, "I would paint you."

"Naked?"

"Possibly."
"You can," Ashley said, "if you want."
"I don't think it would work," I said. "I wouldn't be able to find the right colors."
"That's fine."
"Or I could reinterpret you," I said, "as a triangle."

::::::::::::::::::::

I went on a journey in the forest, not where I'm going. The angles were strange there, not concentric, not setting like themselves. They bent in manners that defied the geometric, bisecting, dissecting, discarding. Triangulating beams lit the night above, glowing odd blue colors. Electricity shot from a gash in the earth. The trees bent, fearful. They were this place, but this was place was something else, not them; skewed inklings quartered the borders of dimension, time and place in destruction. I took steps. This was not a good place to declare everlasting love, nor was it a proper time to write a poem. I had a pen in my pocket but it wasn't important enough to remember. I had my camera but it might not have paid attention.

::::::::::::::::::::

Light bulbs
flaring quiescent
     in the deepest darkest void gaseous clouds reaching out
     and I fell
     down to the center of the universe
     past lakes of hydrogen amitosis and translucent bellied nebuloid creatures
softly scrounging
       in this deepest darkness
at that place where matter cut off and the stars all outside destroying together
        shone
    in synchrony
    together. Still with them I fell
to learn a lesson
    to teach myself what it meant to see
          in secrets,
     whole realms of diffident belief. Still falling
   I came   to a gigantic,
whiteness   the point

Voices

of division   and revolution
around which   all creation
life and   being
   made   circles.
      And no,   it wasn't
         enough   just to
           be here   I wanted
              to really
                BE
                HERE
            in the   gargantuan
          sense,   spreading out,
       garrulously,   from a real,
     provable point,   and onto
an absolute   kind of
the critical.   It was selfish
I know but   who I am
(who am I)   to granulate
     virtue? Life   makes me
        no promises, but very frequently it makes
          choices to
take things away with   and without
       approval, as though
     I had a right to give any, taking one true grasp of reality
and biting
    off a piece larger than the world.
And there I am, cut off from myself, from
         life, from beauty, from whatever individualized form
of mitosis. I'm not
      a cellular structure, but neither am I
     an amoeba, living in my own telephone world, at trigger point,
       swallowing daily a whole carton's worth
    of raw eggs. Not all of us
are meant to be martyrs, and
        even fewer are granted
escape from ghostliness. It's not that I'm selfish, even though I am, but the older I
get, the more of
    the world

I see (very small, one personalized city, destructive),
I want to see less and less; always
coming through
that useless window
that is me, eyes and face, hands in the mirror.
No sound
followed me there:
nexus of quietude, silent, spinning
axis of language. The abstract was meaningless
here, if it distanced itself
from me. The artistic, the unsound. I've got
no right to make claims on creation, unsound, unspoken.
In contradiction, I spoke loudly in the silence, speaking to myself
alone.
There were no voices for me here, no words on the walls.
If existence can be said
to be bound, certainly the concept escaped me. I held my
breath, adrift beneath
the surface of an immense ocean, mirroring the sky
as all creation mirrors
the external, hiding, by means of reflection, its secret of the internal, the silent and
true.
I spoke to myself with many voices, and dampened my
voice on speaking. I had no
concept of loneliness.
Galaxies of color accented a fluctuating, formless
kind of vision.

::::::::::::::::::::::

"If you wanted," I said, "
I could reinterpret you
as language."
(If you wanted, she said,
I could make you
even more
of a liar.)

Voices

::::::::::::::::::::

I looked carefully in the mirror.

    And it was true, I saw.

    A hazing outline, the color of skin. It blurred. I splashed water, crisp and clear, both and neither. I blinked. I thought for a moment of memory.

    It wavered.

                     vision/split.

    There were two(2) of me.

Voices

V

In
s
          i
n
          k
i
          n
g

I am
          an engraving

on the side
of an old,
          beat up,

car

Voices

This is the part where I let you in on a big, big secret, if I can be said to have secrets at all, the outpour that is me, cubist misrepresentation, trace of imagery. It happened so long ago I can't be said to be going in order, but, in all things, I am absolutely untrustworthy.

    Sometimes,
     I can almost rely on myself to preserve
     structure,
but I'm still playing games
with words..
If I were to have a conversation with Pythagoras I would tell him we were all language, even numerically, inasmuch as all that represents is a language in itself. Very likely, in true historical form,
     he would look to murder me.

::::::::::::::::::::

Markus wrung his hands. Markus shook. He didn't want to play video games, and he didn't want to play guitar. No differences cared for him, as the world would have us believe. In the other room, his mother was watching television loudly, as she screamed. She watched with hands clinging (tightly) to the seat, so (tightly) her knuckles went white. The blood could barely squirt through. Vicarious, pathetic, her wasted chorus of representation: any minute now, she would most likely begin to vacuum.

"Do you hear the voices?" he asked, as though confirmation were enough to resolve the whispers away. They hid everywhere, in cupboards, in ceilings, in the walls, nothing we could understand, an undertone to humanity. Silent flickerings in the very domestic safe. They followed us.

"Yeah," I said, "I hear them."

Silent flickerings in the very domestic safe.

They repeated themselves.

"What are we going to do?" he asked. He enjoyed repeating himself. Like everyone, he was entirely a product of his time and place, understanding nothing of self-awareness. The world is fond of making us answer questions, all at once, so the static can get going. Paradoxical, the answers never come through.

"I think it's your camera," he said.

"We've talked about this before," I said. "You know it isn't."

"*You* say it isn't," he said. "That doesn't change anything."

"It isn't," I said, "because I said it isn't. And most of the time, I'm always right"

:::::::::::::::::::::::

"You know," Markus said. "Sometimes I really don't like you."

I didn't care enough to ask him why, but he kept going.

"You're half a person. You've *always* been half a person. You're barely even here."

He didn't notice that (sometimes) I have two shadows.

:::::::::::::::::::::::

Trey came to me in my dreams- not a phantom. I'd fallen asleep in the park, on a bench. Way in the distance, the tops of buildings were an irregular range of mountains. My side hurt, under assault by firmness. Trey seemed excited, but Trey was always excited. He had more energy than a nuclear reactor, despite the strangeness. I hate when people wake me up.

"Are you going tonight?" he asked.

"If I can," I said, "I will."

:::::::::::::::::::::::

"What do you want me to do?" I asked.

"You could do *something*," Markus said, "instead of just standing there. You do that too much." One hand fell on a table. As though he wanted to throw it at me. "You never do anything," he repeated. "You're barely even there."

"I don't even understand what you *want* me to do," I said. "You know no one listens to artists. No one understands them."

"What?"

Voices

(No one listens to artists.)
"I can't hear you."

::::::::::::::::::::::

—Maybe like, speak a little louder, he said.
(I am, I said. You just can't hear me.
)
—What?
(You just can't hear me.)

::::::::::::::::::::::

"Are you scared?" I asked.
"Of course I'm scared," Markus said. "Aren't you?"
"I'm not sure. Maybe. If I know how to be."
"You're just too fond of pretending," he said. "You don't even understand fear."
"I do," I said. "You just don't understand the way I understand things."

::::::::::::::::::::::::

—See? Markus said. You can't stop speaking in riddles, even when it matters. It's like you've fallen out of touch with the real
(You're imagining things, I said.)
He paused.
—What...?
(You're imagining—)
Maybe it was just the vacuum, but he still couldn't hear.

::::::::::::::::::::::

"Are you going to the hill tonight?" I asked. "To watch the fireworks?"
Ashley laid her head on my shoulder. Supine, the Grecian smoothness of her skin, her elegance and elements of posture: she did. With one hand, she played with a ring of keys. This was her car. We were in the wrong seats.
"Maybe," she said. "If you are."
"I am."
Then so am I.

We breathed. I heard her breathing. It surprised me, she always did. To see her chest move. She had a pulse, barely, all up and down her, inside.

"Do you remember Markus?" I asked.

"I do."

(He really likes you.)

"Don't worry," she said. "I'll be nice."

"You don't have to be," I said, "if you don't want to. Unless you feel like it."

"Why do you even talk to him?" she said. "You guys don't match. It's obvious. He follows you, and when you feel like it, you drag him."

"I think he's just more real than I am." She knew. "He does things a real person does."

"He makes you feel better about yourself."

"Absolutely."

"You parasite."

"I am."

We breathed slowly, unsure. The light shone through us, the wind blew through. We filtered dimension. We felt for sure.

She picked up my camera.

"Why do you still have this?" she asked. "It comes between things."

"Yeah," I said. "It does that."

"You don't mind?"

"That's what I have it for."

"But then..." she asked. "Where do you fit in here?"

"I don't," I said. "That's part of the idea."

"Some girls might find that strange."

"Do you?"

"Yes." She touched me. "But I've never been good at finding things"

"I've never been good at seeing."

"It's because sometimes you only have one eye."

"Not quite." I sat up little. "I have three. Just one of them is just better with memory, and it keeps secrets."

She traced a finger over me. She traced elegantly: chest, stomach, thigh. She traced unbelievable. I don't think I knew her very well. However we got here. Wherever we went.

"How many other girls are you with?" she asked.

"Just one," I said. "But she doesn't count. She cancels herself."

"I've heard of her," she said. "Everyone has."

"Are you jealous?"

Voices

"Yes."

"Girls scare me," I said. "Especially you."

"I scare everyone," she said. "It's because I'm scary."

I ran a hand down her spine, in its glorious effeminate curvature, wondering that I could be here, that I could be.

::::::::::::::::::::

Markus stood up. He punched the wall. I'd never seem him this angry before. Whispers surrounded us, whispers became us, all around, in the walls, a spidery

undertone to being, gone unheard. But we heard it, we knew... accumulated dead, a baroque display of memory. Our society, in being so electric, numbs those silent voices- static, flaring noise- but we heard them. They were all of those thing (they were none), I knew, more than Markus. All he knew was how to get angry. That was very

human

of him. Apparently he heard them more than ever.

In another room, his mother was still vacuuming, as she watched TV. He went to her. His house was shit, with strange colors on the walls, and dusty curtains. His mom never did do a very good job keeping it clean. I stepped

over

stains, the maimed remnants of place. Markus raged. She watched television so loud it consumed her. Television had a stifled, fluorescent embrace, like tiredness. His mother got very little sleep. When she did, she slept on the couch, still watching.

Markus stepped into the front room. Next door, the neighbors were pulling into their garage, in a very old, very rusted car. There was a domesticated species of bird perched on the bird feeder. Markus pushed her away from the vacuum. Without turning it off, he lifted it (wobbling) from the ground, and flung it towards the screen. With physics to blame, he fell. The vacuum crashed

t h r o u g h

the television, sparking, as a whole radioactive generation came to an end (with the shredding of wires, undoing internal projection). In silence, to the echo of cracking glass, he landed, gently, on the couch.

::::::::::::::::::::

"This
is all your fault," he said.
        (I felt better about
        myself.

)

::::::::::::::::::::

"Are they telling us something?" Markus asked.
    "They want us to go." Into the dark.
    So we went into the dark. We became familiar with dark places. Markus's basement was very old. Destruction laced pathways to either side. Astringent powder fell from above. Dankness and dampness, the welcomers of memory, were, in their remarkably clammy presence, very prominent. Metal beams, irregular, kept the ceiling up. The naked underbelly of the residence (water heater, sewage pipes, bulbous, rusted tanks of metal) bared itself explicatively, and we saw. It was remarkably disturbing. Like being dumped in a bucket of cold water.
    "What do we do?" he asked, depending on me.
    "Just listen," I said, because there was loudness here.
    And we listened.
From all sides slowly, silently, they came, like a party of old men playing checkers, the sounds of sliding, an ominous undertone. Our God had forgotten to wear a condom; our world was a sick wormhole of semen. I knew then that hundreds of miles away old men in tall hats were shopping for
                        bags of chips and gallons of ice cream at bargain
prices, purchasing swiftly, and with character, less the gremlins come for them. Arrogant creatures with two legs and no sense of gravity left sets of footprints
                    obsessively, for the sake of leaving. We'd
come to it here, in the dark,
        the collective. Lime built up mineral deposits. Gristly strains of gravel
           collected. *The first, with hands, and the other,*
               esophagi.
And then, gloriously, the basement became a mural. Solid color etched the walls. It had the texture of chalk, and it flaked, fluttering as it fell. Size became color, became shape became memory. A tree, resilient in the autumnal wind, struck out at oncoming change, xanthus against searing amber. Farm carts peeling were parked forgotten by the barn. There was a house, strong and proud; a swing; another barn. In the distance a snaking, narrowing path led to town, matted after years of beating.

Voices

There were no animals. Flooding out, a purple wave, tinged different shades along the edge, overwhelmed regularity, and the scene changed to a beach, under the same sky, rocking in the waves. Flat sand and winds. Patches of trees, further up the shore, stood patiently growing; spread back to what might have been a forest. Golden dust sprinkled   Flowing in the. Time, life, dust, ashes, ashes in the dust, flailing, it had scars and hands, faces, darkness. Sewing, with a needle. Old games old old games. It might have been artistic if it weren't so blatantly pathetic: a plea for ongoing sequence. The extrovert crying hydrogen tears.

It wasn't

a mural, it had

never been a mural. I

didn't know

what to

say

.

Big, big clouds stretched

all   across a   space

resembling the sky,

and groggy rain

looked like

it was about to fall

. No, it had a body,

and it

was standing

straight

up.

It had

two   legs,

(one on   each side)

as though it were looking to support itself, this shadow thing,
     scrambling from a platform unto us. Rasping breath escaped it, and laces of blackness collected. Golden rings glowed in the center. It stumbled, unused to existence. It was

a

stranger here, and we feared it. Feeble torso, failing body. It came to life, here in the stagger, and called to us weakly. We heard,

     but we pulled away. It had no arms. It saw we had them, and strove, sprouting appendages. Two. Three. Off balance, it fell.

                    The floor
                          was not kind to frailty, as it was made of
cement,   and it burst to shadow. Black, sagging mist, groping.
             It called
             to us, weaker yet, and we
                                    pretended not to
                    hear.

                    ::::::::::::::::::::

"So you're here?" Trey asked.

"Obviously."

"Did you bring anyone."

"I thought I was bringing Ashley," I said. "Though apparently not."

Up on top of the hill, Markus was already high. Glazed over, he stared, fascinated, at the mystery that was heaven, heaven being somewhere above, if it was. Heaven reminded me of old, old questions. I stood for a while against a tree, thinking. Then, catching a leaf, I tore it in two. Night fell, a gradual dampening in the light. All existence follows the same patterns.

"Wait for me," I said. "I need to find Ashley."

"The sky won't wait for you," Trey said. "You know that."

"Hey man," Markus said, "stay here... we've got... we've got earplugs, and whiskey, and a mag-nifying glass." He waved them. He had all three- though there were actually two magnifying glasses, one for each eye, glass goggles for ogling the sky. Ogling

is such a strange word. Its meaning escapes me.

"It's fine," I said. "She said she'd be here."

Trey shook his head.

"Sometimes," he said, "you really aren't such a great guy. Always ditching us for girls." Sounding so adolescent, unsurprisingly, like a teenage boy, half drunk, wearing goggles and sitting outside on a hill to watch the fireworks. He fit in, irrevocably, with himself.

"It's fine," I said. "Sometimes I'm really *not* a good guy."

Don't be giving me your sympathy, he said. *If you're going to be like that, just don't come back. We don't want you here. Inside, we know you're nothing but the shadow of a shadow.* In the light.

"Maybe I'll come back," I said. I found myself wondering who Trey was. I don't think I'd ever seen him before.

Voices

::::::::::::::::::::::

"It's trying to stand," I said. Markus was too afraid. In our dark the shadows moved. It had flesh of spuming ash. Its existence was agonizing pain. I realized I'd been here before, or it seemed like I had. I'd painted this scene before, so many times, without painting. And I knew this ghost. I'd shaken his hand.

Markus tried to run. I held him back.

"Can you hear?"

But, facing forward, here where the whispers became accumulation, excess drove him to deafness. He was deaf and blind, in weakness. Gravity pressed his skull against the ground. Repression dumped him in a pool of hardening grease. He broke the surface with a plunge, making the crust flake, but drank sickness, a pooling brown color, like shit. The muck flung handfuls and he sank.

Torrid breath, scentless, stained the cement. Wilting and crying. Dissipating smoke curled off limbs, like a cigarette with no filter, wasting away, in pollution. Contraceptive energies ricocheted within, stretching the torso. It gave birth to a death-baby, amniocentesis to end all sleeping, it nurtured itself poorly, in all ways absolutely at odds with the real: built up of silent voices. Hardness platformed decay. Putrefaction prefigures death.

::::::::::::::::::::::

"You probably shouldn't have come," Ashley said.

"But you promised," I said, "that you would be there."

"I can lie," Ashley said. "I'm a liar."

"If that's what you say." I held her hand. "Why didn't you come?"

"I didn't feel like it."

"You didn't want to see me?"

"Yes."

"Why."(not a question)

"Because you'll just be thinking about her."

"Not true."

"You're right, it's not."

"Then what?"

"Didn't feel like it."

"Whatever," I said. "If you want, you can lie to me."

"It's fine," she said. "I already have."

I stood with her for awhile. The trees blocked out sound. Thirty feet away, Trey and Markus saw through new sets of eyes. I didn't have to go far.

"If you want," I said, "you can leave."

"I'll stay," she said. "I want to see the fireworks."

As I held her, she felt absolutely, remarkably unreal. Above, the sky split, letting pour its great reserve. Brightness spiraling. Under the roar, I heard Trey scream, as though he'd been launched into space, atop a nuclear missile. Pirouettes of unbalance showered on high, hanging in sus-pension. I smiled, and thought of writing a poem. I wasn't on a hill, and they weren't the right colors, but it was almost as though the stars were falling for me.

Voices

The
b   r   i   d   g   e
was still here. There was still
very little flowing.

"I was wrong," I said, raising a hand. "About you."
"That's because..." the man with the afro might never have left, *"it must
be because
you're a horrible person."*

"Maybe."
"You throw rocks at small animals," he said,
*"and
you have a big piece of
garlic in
your soul."*

"You're one to talk," I said. "You can't even speak straight."
(in straight lines)
He straightened.
*"W
h
a
t
does that matter
?"*

"I never said it did."

I laughed
and said:
"I don't apologize very often."
"You
aren't

doing

a very good job
right now."

"Why not?"

"You made me d
a   *n*

c

e

" he said. *"You can*
NEVER
apologize
for that."

I shrugged. "Well at least I tried," I said.
"And what can I say?
I thought you looked like a dancer."
He wretched, picking
his nose.
"At least I think I understand you now," I said.
"You're like an artist, just not a very good one."

::::::::::::::::::::

I led, with James leading, (along) a concrete stream, glass fish swimming, electric animals eating (shitting repeating)(blood shit tufts of fur) in the groves at either side, looking at us as we led, out innocent, opalescent eyes. He skipped, fluting, and I played a game of catch with myself. The idea had something phallic about it, as long as it was still tied to language. Up above: flat clouds in a soft fading sky, around a nub of color in the center, dull pink folded to a pastel painted clitoris. Evening paved the city in dusk. Fire fell when the sun shut its eye.

"The city's sick," I said.
James, beside, walked with his head down.
"Yeah," he said, "I know."

"Seriously," I said, "we're so sick. Every day, it's all I can do to keep from sacrificing babies. I hate these people so much they're going to make my eyes fall out. We're so sick.
        Seriously."
"It's always been this way," James said.
"Of all people,
I would
            probably
know."

::::::::::::::::::::

Markus sat with me by the edge of the sea. We sat out. We were. We would drink the waves; we would split the horizon. That's not right. Really. For being rock, centuries broken into a million dirty fragments, baked, split open, mauled, cut into by rain and weather, beating incessant for a million years, in packs, in stretching planes, the sand was surprisingly gentle. I remembered.
"The sea's hungry," I said. "It wants to swallow us whole."
"No," Markus said, "it hungers for the shore."
"Same thing."
"It doesn't care about us."
"Whatever," I said. "The ocean doesn't do so well with barriers. It's breaking through the water. These things
    go both
    <-----
    directions
        ------->
."

::::::::::::::::::::

"Jesus," he said. "Your neighbor. She's dead."
    "It's fine," I said. "It's what she wanted."
Laying
    there
    bent over, white with maggots in her skin, uglier than in life almost; flabbing slab and breasts together; her neck bent to an impossible angle by death, chin coated in what might be drool: she had the breath of a corpse, still coming, as

stagnancy swept through her, slowly, with the time she gave it; splayed hands on the couch; she had a thread of yarn in one hand, claws in either direction extended, and by the fire a trail of fire burned slowly up the length to what might have been a (blazing) sweater, mass produced, one and one, and imbued by her with a whole lifetime's worth of resentment, not to mention deceptively poor insulation. In time, the flame would get to her. She was a burner of witches.

 "Lets get out of here," I said. "I have no idea why we came."

:::::::::::::::::::::

"I don't know

           if you'll believe

      me,"

   I said
    "but

      there

   are 2

              (

      two)

   of me

   ...and
  she wasn't
      there

  alone.
   "

Voices

I walked with James. Maybe that was just because I didn't care where we were going. These days I have trouble keeping aware of time. There were so many people here and so many of them were exactly the same. No surprises. We fed our inner animal things the bacteria hadn't gotten to yet- very little. Disorientation, a sense of spreading, gives off ripples of motion.

"I'm hungry," I said.

"Do you have any money."

I said I didn't.

"Then shut up."

We kept walking. He turned into an alley. I knew this place. The sights, sounds, smells, were little pieces of sickness. It didn't smell right. Puddles of oil, black as month old shit, infested; trash, old papers, cups with nothing in them, missing a side. It was foul here, as death. James brought me here too often. He was turning into an arbiter of destruction.

I stopped him with one hand.

"We can't go back here," I said. "You know that."

"Are you afraid?"

"You owe me."

"He's your fault."

   "I wont, you know. Never."

"I know."

"I've gone back too many times already," I said. "I've gone back there before."

"I know."

I turned around. James played dangerous games. This would never be a good place to write poetry.

::::::::::::::::::::

I knocked on the door. Fly patches flew, zapping in the lantern. Late nights take life and defeat it. He opened fat and bald, ugliness, drenched in ugliness, grease all over his upper lip, long twining hairs beneath his shirt. He chewed rudely. Somewhere within, I felt mildly offended. He smelled like grated cheese.

"Hello," I said.

"Who are you?" He chewed.

"I just wanted you to know," I said, "I'm the guy who broke your mailbox. And I like to write big, colorful poems. The offensive kind. That no one understands."

He looked at me blankly. He chewed. Any second he was sure to give me fury.

"You're that kid that came by with the video camera."

"I am."

"I let you meet my daughter."

"I have."

Gunk bespectacled him. Thick bushels of hair sprouted dualistic, one from each nostril. Fat must be slapping to deafness.

Just a minute ago, I'd broken his new mailbox.

Quakes of anger rumbled in him. He glared.

"Why did you come back?" he demanded.

"Because last time," I said, "you didn't understand."

::::::::::::::::::::

The alley smelled strange. No wind blew here, where it smelled like shit, where the spiders were. By the wall: a carcass leering. On some level I felt overwhelmingly evil, if I could call myself things. I longed to see the sky, not so much for peace, but a reminder of longing. Humidity is an obstacle to passing. This was not a pleasant place to possess a nose.

"Jacob?" I wondered, mocking myself.

But he was there.

Overrun,

grotesque, a nest of spiders. They crawled through tunnels in his ears, fucking with eight legs the depths of his intestines. Arachnid colonies swarmed in him, licking crusted remnants of blood, nibbling at veins. They'd chewed away his eyes, along the stems leading back (narcoleptic), not the mention the spongy mass of his brain. He had no kidneys, no lung and liver. He shat a steady stream of spiders, legs coalescing at a symmetry point, slowly through the very pores in his skin, still gleaming whatever epidermic remnants, liquid leavings to sick weaving muscle. At the very center, in his chest, a wicked, hairy beast with sixteen legs and fifty eyes worked appendages all throughout him, poking at soft things. It fed off cycles of venom, recycling.

"Jacob?" sat by the dumpster, against it; sack and skin, slimed to the metal. Unseeing, he stared. His sockets were pits of spiders. They'd eaten away his clothes, shot venom in his soul. Working diligently, they laced him in webbing, tying down limbs. Most probably, he ached: of vultures and sin.

He moaned.

You,

> *did*

> *this to me.*

If I could think of him as making a sound. With one arm barely raising, he pulled and wanted to point, a long breaking fingernail. He struggled, vomiting streams of spiders. Some made eight legged escapes from cranium, spreading concentric from the center, crawling.

"Jesus," I said, and realized, once and for all. "I thought you got away, but you never even left." The world didn't have room for him, erasing. It came with one eye and false, false reasons, making shit excuses, to chase the wretch away. "I always knew it," I said. "You weren't worth a try."

He moaned. From either side he'd sprouted the beginning of four new arms. When they were done he would have eight legs. Achromatic down, gossamer, covered him. He shook in pain. Across his forehead a gash split open. The skin slid away over a red eye. He saw the world the color of blood. Heated, unfriendly. In unification, we hated him.

> *I know*

what

> *you're*

thinking, he said.

> > (I hated him)

> > > In the life.

> He was sickening

as

> wet dirt
> sprouting worms

> > > in

> the rain.
> He gaped with one evil eye.
> The dumpster flew at me.

::::::::::::::::::::::

James took me with him to a concert. In concert places the kids were my age. They had long hair and wore very strange clothing. They danced. Pyrotechnics wove blazing discoloration, flitting brilliantly on a crooked shoulder, the flatness, shadowing the bridge of the nose. In moving they culminated to an absolute mass of randomness, in unification.

The band sucked. They wasted space on the stage.

"Lets get out of here," I said. "You know I can't stand concerts anymore."

"Yeah," he said, "I know."

::::::::::::::::::::::

He yelled at me.
No, language can't capture such
disfigurement.
He shook his fist, shot spittle, and bulged uncontrollably.
Still,
he didn't realize
                    I'd already gotten
                                        his
mailbox.

::::::::::::::::::::::

Inhaling, I dived. It was something like a commando roll, just I wasn't a commando. I landed on shards of broken glass. Still sliding (and quickly), the dumpster buckled, the hull throbbed, and it belly flopped against the wall. Handfuls of trash flung into the air- a mass of mothball, plastic bags, drain cleaner, rotten fruit, dirty boxes- and bounced against the wall. They made a wet, sopping sound, that had different layers in it; bringing to mind simultaneously puddles of rain and flushing toilets; and fell all together, with the patter of wrung paper towels, thumbing at the bottom. Flecks of blood escaped me. I cringed.

He raised an arm, still gasping. Tunnels opened all atop his cranium, and his skull became a pin-cushion of swirling, whirling eyes. They swept, squinting for image. He saw in all directions panoramic. A wave scuttled to me. They made crackling sounds. I found myself wishing I'd brought a hefty jar of poison.

Voices

At all sides, concrete cracked. Directly in front, a slab tore free, rocking the walls. He'd cornered me as a consequence of poorly understood mathematical function, calculoid symmetries yielding ratios pertaining to the capabilities of the human body in unfamiliar situations, gauging reaction time breathing heart rate and muscle stipulations. Even now, disfigured, he understood nothing of self awareness.

The slab was five feet high. Rushing, it tore to me, tide breaking stone, sweating dull powder to either side. It had a face, oh yes: flatness and old markings in the sedimentary skin, unseeing, unthinking. It rushed. The garbage hadn't been touched in almost half a year. It made me wish I was made of a fortified grade of titanium, the unbreakable kind, that had none of the weakness of skin, though maybe I could afford to go with steel.

I climbed. The dumpster, still there, provided height, at exact odds to uselessness. Lunging, I lipped the top and passed it over, unbelievably touching the top with the back of one leg. Until now, I'd never thought of myself as being made of water. In the most strenuous of situations, I surprise myself.

::::::::::::::::::::

The mountains
　　　　were rough as
　　granulated
　　　　steel
　　　　on the way up, though the higher I got
it gave way to the slickness
　　　　of icy cold, numbing the tips of fingers.
　　　　　　　I could
　　manage to pull myself
because I was strong, apparently,
　　　　　　　　　　　though
　　　　　　　　I'd never thought of myself
　　　　　as being strong
　　　　　before.
Up above,
　　　the moon
was
　　　very
　　　large.

119

:::::::::::::::::::

In tiredness, he choked. Dead spiders lie to either side, flattened against the wall, pasted to a layer of fleshy juice, searing in venom. Evacuating strains poured from him, a million scraping legs. They made webs in direction, taking to the walls, an arachnoid spreading. Stumbling, I took hold of a cylindrical molding, composed mainly of iron, which in more casual times I might have referred to as a pipe, if not for the juvenile connotations. Looking out (two hollow, outflowing sockets and fifty red holes), he feared me.

sWINGING

I lopped him through the face, cutting horizontal past the brittle shield of bone. Visage came untangled. His skull hit a wall, still flying, and buckled to the ground. Fifty crimson miniatures acclimated to him, dislodged. They were red. Their backs bore bleeding eyes. They crawled from tiny holes, wriggling all over. They gasped for breath in the merciless outside.

From Jacob's opening sprang something covered almost entirely in eyes and hair. It had sixteen legs and clung with them, letting go sounds of squishing flesh, merciless parasitism. It probed his ears, clung through them; set staves through nose and mouth, staring at me. The whole bulbous mass of it writhed, a vilified strain, destructive.

:::::::::::::::::::

Stabbing
    with the pipe,
        I pegged
     it
     to the wall
       behind.

Voices

These
            people were sick, and their campfires were a mess of bleeding horseflesh
and badly tended crops. Sickly grinning, they wore masks
                        of hollow leather skin that never stopped grinning. In conjunction,
the   whole evil lot of them, they
            laughed together, dumping blood drawings
                        on canvasses made of the same leathered skin.
            Looking down, from atop
a high mountain, I
            saw them all at once, taking in their stench.
                        They smelled like
            a world without a shower, tasted
                                    like the droppings of an infected animal
about to die, laying
            at midday in a sweating
            pool of sun, green ooze
                        pouring
                        from the gaps
            in its skin.
                                    The mountain in its harshness,
rebuked me, by
            setting obstacles,
                        by
            hurling dangers, but I have
no fear of coldness, that that which remembers
            the emptiness
                        at the origin of the soul, unmoving in itself,

as all around, niched in the center of the universe,

a

brocade of lights
broke out swirling
to swallow all
sense of center, *a howling dip*
in the archways.
I climbed, squinting, and the mountain
fed me the remains
of old bones.
Licking white remnants, I grew,

(tiring)

ever closer
to the moon.

::::::::::::::::::::

She wasn't there alone.
(That's not to say.)
She took my world and refracted it, laced furiously in pandemic voices. She gave me
fury, and I traced it back to her, my epidemic queen, she was, we danced all
night in cool moonlight, and talked about meetings, about rain.
The police came for us, but we were already gone. And even though people
told stories about her, unless I believed in them, very few, if any, were true.
With her I was a vilified, expressionist sort, of their, the kind who couldn't
help but grasping
for a taste of absolute beauty. Her formlessness, her voluptuous sense of
the awesome, dug tunnels in me, and let flow a whole
purifying infinity outflow, rushing water
carving routes of drainage all into, out of my lungs. She made me less, made me
more   than human, by
humoring me. As of now, I'd seen her thrice (once in life, again in refraction, and a
precursor in dreams) and all three times,
she'd never
been alone.

::::::::::::::::::::

Voices

"I need to find her."

James held my shoulder. He said I really shouldn't.

"And you're going to help me," I said, "because you know where she's at."

That might be true.

"If you find her," he said, "he'll send them for you."

"And if I wait," I said, "he'll come for me himself."

James sighed. He stuck a hand in his pocket. Loud music from another room assaulted us. I was in the mood for loud music. Detached from the personal, it soothed me.

"If you tell me," I said, "I'll paint a huge banner of you in real colors all over main street, so no matter where you look, people will see you, and, without being, you can be everywhere at once."

"You're funny."

"I know."

"But really," he said. "Why do you tell such strange lies?"

"Because I've been spending too much time with girls," I said, "and they've been teaching me how to lie."

"You're funny," he repeated.

"I know."

:::::::::::::::::::::

In a subway somewhere, in an old station where the rails don't work anymore, my train was getting ready for me.

I know.

You shouldn't say things like that so often.

:::::::::::::::::::::

He screamed. I poked him in the stomach, a barrel of blubber.

He heaved. He said the world was hell already. His daughter came down the stairs, looking afraid. She was small, her clothes were small, and her breasts were small. She stood holding a blanket, looking absolutely, unspeakably afraid. Her nose wiggled, and her eyes squinted. All her life, her father had taught her to be afraid.

Still screaming, he muted himself. It wasn't that he was too ferocious, or even too stupid. This place was completely unremarkable. The longer I stood there the more I wondered if I could get away with hitting him. I had a pipe with me. A camera. Neon juxtapositions clouded electron gaping space. When he spoke, I wanted to make pretentious literary jokes about silence.

::::::::::::::::::::

"You know," James said. "Sometimes, I just don't understand you."

"What is there to understand?"

"For one, how you can ask that question when you ask it so often, and so furiously, that there are two of you, and you don't have any shadow."

"I've told you before," I said. "It's because I like to play games with words."

::::::::::::::::::::

I climbed.

In the morning, to escape the storm, I holed up in a cave. Water dripped from the ceiling. Soon it would become a spear of ice, pointing cold fingers at the ground. It was too cold for anything natural to be living in here. I lit a fire and failed to thaw myself. Blue lines ate my skin. Freezing tendrils tore me.

To chase the boredom away, I wrote a poem
cold colorless lives in the echelon dusk
winking words silent shaking loudly feeding
the lies blatant hiding I shout quietly
at the backs of animals they ignore me
always so caught up in an empty
kind of life the animal
is nothing but fur and baking skin the innards
go moving as the bones shuffled across gruff
gruff gruff is the hard living really I wonder
how the mountain treats gofers without ever
coming around to fall it ignores the seasons
really I guess it has the right to ignore it's own
the icicles are growing tonight cold in the
very depth of mountain caves firelight the
scent of melting water steaming drizzling up
to join a fluffing cloud in the sky
hands folding coolly over ligaments
tendons and whatever curling pieces
of bone
but stopped halfway in, for boredom.

Voices

He's ready for you.
     "Tell him I'm not interested."
Then you'll
                    hear
     from him soon.

:::::::::::::::::::::

For some reason, I seem to be talented at making enemies in high places who come thundering with fury of the whole goddamn searing sky (throwing fire, knocking down buildings) and despite brief feelings of coolness the whole situation just really doesn't appeal to me.

But it doesn't matter. I need to find her.

:::::::::::::::::::::

"You owe me," I said. "You do."

James laughed, flipping a coin. He had other people to pay his debts. We both knew. I'm not sure why I bothered. Maybe he was playing with me.

"She's not here," he said.

"What?"

"If she was here," he said, "I would know. But I looked everywhere for you-" all over the city, on top of buildings, under bridges, in the park, very old restaurants where not even the regulars show up anymore; secret hangouts, alleyways, clubs, public school buildings, hideouts, cheap, scummy business that deal under the table in types of business the police probably want to know about; playgrounds, movie theaters, dead end streets, video stores; and last, for the sake of completion, hidden places where not even the most privileged eye can see- "and she still isn't there."

"That's not true," I said. "It couldn't be."

"I'm not sure." James said. "I'm not sure if she was ever here."

"People talk about her," I said.

"People talk about everything."

"Wherever I've been," I said, "she's been there. And if I want to go anywhere, she's been there too."

"That's what people say."

"I can find her."

"I can't help you."

"If you say so."

::::::::::::::::::::

The wolves
      were there, in caves. Feral eyes glowed in the darkness. Tight constricted haunches held them, claws in the
          earth. Walking quickly, impatiently, they paced
    from side to side. They had no reason to sit quietly.
         Their
           fur
  was thickly
       tangled.

::::::::::::::::::::

The streets were quiet tonight, to make me think. In windows, stagnancy shifting, beating silently against the walls. I'm not sure if I knew where I was going. I listened to myself: footsteps, rustles, breathing. Too much of my life seems to be a chronicle of breath. Under the light, I studied the absence of my shadow.
    Stain,
  the girders and
    the archways, plotting screaming
grinding
for the furious
    They
were coming. It wasn't that I heard them, or smelled them, or sensed with some gratuitous grasp of position, but they had an aura all their own, the kind that makes me contradict myself. Sometimes I wonder if I'm even worthy of poetry when at times like this I can't even get a grasp of sensation, that tingle at the back of the neck, glowing. I thought of running. At the moment I didn't feel like it. I felt too much like a tired half empty pseudo poet walking through a dark street at odds with very obvious very imminent danger: the kind that had teeth. I meant that to be a metaphor, to misrepresent (in representation), but here I am, getting absolutely confined to the real. Sometimes I frustrate myself.

::::::::::::::::::::

I slept

Voices

for the night
       in a house
       made
       out of snow. It was
very cold, which meant paradoxically, despite the warmth,
       I couldn't touch
              the walls. Not
              only
          would they collapse, destructively,
     but they were
          my absolute coldness
                here, impeding impassive
          to keep
    the wind away.
    It wasn't
          as though
    I believe in taking shelter, but I
          didn't
              have any other choice.
     The mountain
was evil, not as a matter of intent, but as
         a symbol, it leered, intimidating.
                 It threw
              avalanches at me, and snow. I couldn't
         get to the stream
             because it was frozen, and I couldn't go
down
         because
           I was frozen
             too.

         ::::::::::::::::::::

I found her in the darkness, but
   she ran from me.

         ::::::::::::::::::::

I had dreams about visiting the subway. Somewhere within I'd always known I was a summoner of trains. They smiled to me, with two lights. The subway was the circulatory system of the city. Trains were its blood, pumping steal, compartments of flesh. The gods of the subway only came out at night. Somehow, many of them knew me.

From outside, the subway was a gateway into darkness, with a set of stairs leading into it, rails to keep you from falling. Inside the platform was dark. There were advertisements on the wall, featuring beautiful women. They had nothing human about them, no sense of the fallible. Square tiles and coldness, lines in the tiles, each magnified the sound of footsteps. If there were a ghost conductor, he would probably hear me.

The lights came on. The train was already ready. In restraint, like a gigantic, wormoid arrow, it coiled unsleeping, polished steal in the belly of the artificial monstrosity. Most probably I would be the only passenger.

I sat down. My train was remarkably comfort-able. If I hadn't been on a quest I might have written poetry.

:::::::::::::::::::::

I sat on my hill staring at the stars. Unmoving as a consequence of perspective, barely burning, they sat buried in graves of dark matter and blackness. No, they would never fall for me. Each possessed its own significance, but lost itself in the trappings of sky, paling comparison: such, the consequence of context, of togetherness and implications, they defeated each other, not some advocate of silent burning. They spoke to me implicitly by making cerebral patterns in the light.

:::::::::::::::::::::

He

had me walking along a long carpet. The carpet was red (velvet maybe, to make awkward guesses, though I've never claimed to be an encyclopedia of material), and there was nothing to see beyond it. Very possibly if I stepped off I would fall. The void is not a good place to spend vacation, the void is not conductive to the expression of truth. Such spaces between the real: useless in themselves, that which isn't. The only ones who care to go there are the dead, and they don't

care.

He gave me

Voices

a golden light at the end of the carpet, unflattering. Obviously he had a fondness for parody. If I'd had had an inclination to the obtuse, the slapstick and crude, I might have found it
amusing.

:::::::::::::::::::::::

Two weeks after she left, I found Veronica's body slumped in a dumpster somewhere. In death she defied description. I wished we'd run away to the desert.

:::::::::::::::::::::::

The conductor was a nice old man despite the fact that I could see through him. He had a voluminous white mustache that danced as he spoke. In bulk, he filled the compartment, and by extension a very large sterile blue uniform. As we spoke parts of the train spiraled into smoke. Sitting in the back cars, too distracted to write poetry, I'd found this pass-ably interesting. On some seats could be seen the smoking remnants of passengers. I could hear the echo of conversation (an auditory dimness), not to mention the sounds of shuffling. Out the window there was very little: scenery intermingling blackness. I had no idea where we were going. Phantom trains are famous for having mysterious destinations. Mine was no exception.

"Hey," I said. With both hands, he turned knobs, switched switches, pulled pulleys. I got the impression it was a decorative gesture, for my sake. His hat sat steadily perched, the same blue as his uniform.

"Any idea where we're going?"

"The train decides these things."

"This your first run?"

"And last," he said. "Someone up high must think you're really important."

"Yeah," I said. "I am."

I stood against the wall, still watching windows. Brief flickers: the park at midday, the inside of a college student's apartment, a department store, alleyways, cafes where not even the poets understand poetry. Ripples in the wall. Unsurprisingly, very few things in the train were not the color of metal.

"I used to have a family," he said. "A long time ago."

"Are they still around?"

"My grandchildren are."

"Oh," I said. "I'm sorry."

"It's not so bad."

"I'm glad."

"Sometimes though-" I don't think I'd noticed before now, but he was smoking a very large, very brown cigar, puffing clear smoke- "if I ever had the chance to talk to the Big Man, if there is such a thing, I would tell him just to get rid of the whole thing."

"Death?"

"Life. It doesn't work very well."

"Oh," I said. "Okay."

"There's not really so much to miss, when you think about it." Outside the window I saw the flash of a basketball court. It reminded me of Travis. I hadn't thought of him in a very long time. "Just because people tell you there is, most people do. It's another one of society's lies. Barbecues, television, hours every day on a train. It's not so great. And neither are the people."

I itched my left arm.

"I outlived my wife," he said. "And my daughter."

"I'm sorry."

"Don't be," he said. "I didn't love them. And you aren't really sorry. You just think you are, because people say you ought to be." I didn't interrupt him. He was right. "These things get so much clearer after you're gone," he continued. "Before, I was a very happy man."

"Do you ever see them anymore?"

He said he didn't care, which made sense.

"Just make sure wherever you're going," he said, "after you get there don't think it matters so much what you do. Happiness, sadness, love and death. You're nothing but the echo of an echo. We all learn that one day."

::::::::::::::::::::

When

I reached the end of the carpet, I found him waiting for me. Immediately I didn't like him. He shoes shined too bright, his teeth gleamed with too much whiteness. He didn't understand that suits and greased hair aren't cool anymore. In the true spirit of self servitude, he sat on a huge golden throne, burnished, that in comparison made him look small, but functioning as an extension of himself, meant to act as a signifier of magnificent golden presence. He wore sunglasses, and tipped them to me. I bet if he were to refer to them, he would call them *shades*.

"I'd just like you to know," he said, "that every time you met her, no matter what you thought, she was never alone." In one hand he held a long thin black cane.

Voices

At one end it had a sculpture of something."I just figured I should give you a fair warning," he said, flashing eyes, "because I'm a fair guy, sometimes. That I'm coming for you." His suit had very few creases in it.

"It's fine," I said. "I'm a fighter."

"I've also heard that you're a liar."

"You're right," I said. "I am."

:::::::::::::::::::

I ran back for her in the forest, almost falling in the mud. Above, in the canopy, leaves cut a lattice through the moon, and drooped over the path, off heavy wet branches. Inhalation sheared paths in shadow. In one hand I held my palm, in the other my camera. It hurt without: diatomic, a soul deep splitting, way down where I wasn't me anymore, inside; optiod linkage, plastic and glass, tying me to me, the absence of my own shadow. In the dark, I doubt she noticed.

I broke through the woods, parting dark green curtains. Orange flashes, clouds of unfiltered smoke. There were no sirens, but residual eruptions refracted the flow, taking time and replaying it. Where I was, if I could be here. Hearing sounds, kissing beautiful girls in the rain. I leaned against a tree, to catch my breathing. She wasn't there, but she was still leaving.

(
Even though it was raining, we never
went inside.)

:::::::::::::::::::

Flashes of mirage in the belly of the desert; cool clears pools gleaming my sacred oasis. I slept in the cold at the side of the bay, head in hands. Gentle pillows of sand, bearing an aforementioned history, staggeringly unimportant, lofted me to dreams. The desert made marking on dry baked skin. I slept with sand in my hair, dust in my throat, echoes of brightness still burning. In the dream I had a vision of a
sandstorm.

It came at me a whirlwind of heaviness, granulated flying. Underneath, in a sandy womb, I saw darkness and bones of dead animals, sapped by the infinite thirst of an overextending desert. Cactus spines joined them, old meat, giving weapons to the storm. Ahead on either side, in the back, the wind picked up, turning abstract shape to flat patterns in the sand, a maternal *lifting up* of body. *When*

I woke up, I took a drink of water, packed my bags, and discovered I was a prophet.

::::::::::::::::::::

The wolves came for me
    when I turned a corner. In the empty streets, I heard them coming (clawed paws scraping holes in the path, five six seven of them coming, red eye, worms in their fur). Somewhere in me, I thought of running. They surrounded, a sacrificial circle. Each had one eye, a geometric anchor to plain, expressing purpose. They growled: yellow teeth, a poisonous tongue.
    I took to the walls,
    to rooftops
    and highness, climbing up windows, hanging down an awning. Sometimes I astound myself with my own agility. If I had friends, maybe I would be able to depend on them to help me. Apathetic, I kicked at teeth and knocked them away. I still
        had the pipe. Though
    it hadn't necessarily been destined to become weaponry, I had the power to alter fate. Gazillions of years ago (to forgo measurement), I'd seen this very thing in dreams. Fur, teeth, claws and bleeding. I was not bleeding, though in all likelihood I ought to be. Metal has the strength to break teeth. I have the power to move metal, inclined to a certain avant-garde sense of the moving.

::::::::::::::::::::

I saw her
    turning a corner, or she was something like her. She had the inward sense of body, the extrovert aura of presence. Dark hair, of more than one color, differentiating, moved in the absence of wind to move it. She walked carefully, and slowly, though no matter how fast I ran she was always so far ahead.

::::::::::::::::::::

A cloaked man, bearing sickness, wearing rags, came to my place in the center of the desert. Scalding winds dug blisters in his skin. Impurity spawned serpents in his blood. Rough cloth cloaking, too thick, fanned to an overarching length behind. Standing thirty feet away, as was custom, he addressed me.
    "I can't help you," I said. "Go away."

Voices

There is no safety under the shadow of this red rock.
    (come sit with me under
    the shadow of this red rock)
"I'm so sick," he said.
""Go away."
"At least pray for me," he said.
"I won't pray."
"But look at what I am!" as he removed the turban, tearing green stained bandages, his rotted skin. "I'm dying!" he ripped gauze bloody red sprouting sickness, calloused, pussed, infected. The skin might as well be falling. So mangled, it came off in strips.
Look at me, cried wounds, we *beg...*
"There's nothing I can do."

::::::::::::::::::::::

Footsteps make such strange sounds (beating beating). They come in sync, signaling movement. Wherever I go, they follow me, like a theme song. Identical, mine and others.
    I followed her. She made no footprints. Her hair billowed as she ran, floating up behind. It reminded me in a way of the first short story I'd ever written, somewhat plagiarized. It was based loosely on footsteps and chasing. In all things, I see my own future, separated from the real, my life running (not exactly) backwards, from the center of time, not slipping in sequence
      what pray pray for me   there's nothing
  I can do
  to help you

::::::::::::::::::::::

I don't know if I
would ever
admit
this to anyone,
but
I can't
even help
myself.

::::::::::::::::::

When the sandstorm came, I found her at its center. She was at the center of all things, not as a kind of focus, but maintaining distance from all points, asymptotically receding. Always slipping, she was there but she never came closer. Everything saw her, always there, even caught fragmented pieces of imagery, but she alludes confinement in representation, canceling herself.

Bathing in
sand, suspending in desert
hands, she was there but not really there. She would not lead me to any dependable source of water, no niche of coolness in the dry ache of the abyss. She laughed, suspended, and beckoned to me. In the eye of the hurricane, surrounded on all sides by walls of earth, taking a step, I barely kept from falling.

::::::::::::::::::

Writing poetry
in the dirt *sweat dust heat*
rock rock beauty in the sand
collapsing

::::::::::::::::::

If I were to have a mantra, it would go something like this (avoiding by careful measures the confines of language, clusters of meaning and often tapped expression- much the kind seen on television, in windows, on *huge* boards off the side of the road- and capturing fully the intricate operation of fern, telephone, barbed wire, bed cushion [not fluffy], and pouring grains of wheat the

::::::::::::::::::

I came out of the subway somewhere near the gateway to the sea. On the horizon, a full globed sun split the water, barrier to barrier rocking wavefronts away. I shifted my shoe in the sand, thinking of ways to capture scenery, its second self, the more important half. I still captured things with my camera. Confined them. Overlapping vision, quinine plausibility of secrets; pen and paper, ink, lines falling irregularly to sequence; separating idea from vision, self and self image, clear filtered projection. Standing against the sky, I had only one shadow. A family, way down the beach, walked along the strand, so dark I couldn't see them. Perspective shore tunnels of vision, rays of lights, sinking in the darkness, they walked along the sea. Irrevocable, in violation of sinking. The sun sank towards the horizon, breaking in half, to vilify night and day.

:::::::::::::::::::::

The subway let me out somewhere in the center of the city. Maybe I could find her here. Slabs of concrete jutted at irregular angles, breaking windows. Stolen merchandise, the useless kinds, fell unstolen, my silent personalized city. Plastic mannequins, still wearing dresses, brassieres, all out on display, were the closest thing I could see to women. Up above, clouds of broken glass, suspended in time, multiplied individual shades of evening. Sky scrapers were caught in falling. Darkish gold, a fire glowing, solid stillness solid marking, enshrouded reflective edges, illuminating emblems of destruction, a pristine pathway.

I took a step forward. I'd seen this place before. Certain paths led certain places, maze-like. My dream city. Bright colors flung banners on high. Smashed in cars asphalt peanuts littering the sidewalk. It smelled like subtlety and extension, an indescribable brink on the senses. I followed myself into the street. By where I was standing, a set of stairs in the street, bleached white, led into the sky. They were white, marble. I approached them. They led to a maelstrom of gravity, an undulating sea of crushing force, heaxi-directional.

I climbed.

And it should have been impossible, but until I got the top, breaking through clouds in the sky, moving towards the moon, there was very little sense of falling.

:::::::::::::::::::::

Blooming *blooming* I spotted a desert rose, calamitous.
It was the kind that shouldn't be growing in the desert, the beautiful kind. It's petals
were dark, pure redness, an elegant blooming, sprouting defiantly here
where not even the strongest flowers grew, still
swaying in the wind, subtly,
just so that
I took
not
ice
of
it
the
st
e
m
glistening with the unmistakable shadings of weaponry. Sharp, <u>shadowy</u> thorns,
acting always in defense of beauty, with prickling tips all along a path leading down
to the

      r   o   o   t   s

(Perfect beauty
in a desert rose.
Pristine
petals
clandestine

destiny)

::::::::::::::::::::

A great beast
rose out of the sea. It had scaled skin, big claws, and inconceivably large teeth.
It broke
the surface with a wave, thrashing out: and a roar,
over
arching,
that most probably could be heard all throughout the city. Taller than a
building, it scraped the sky.
If

Voices

      I were attempting to be
      (contrite)
allusive, I would say it had multiple heads, red skin,
         three numbers etched on its forehead, a body
         composed of many
                  different animals, a clear voice
                that
could speak
      a large #
      of human languages, but that wasn't true.
         From this distance, despite
      contradiction, it could most probably
only
         talk to snakes,
      and it was barely
      thirty
      feet tall.

               ::::::::::::::::::::

When I got to the top of the mountain, a *b*
                         e
                         a
                         m
                      of light came to me, and I looked down at
the whole anonymous world, possibly asleep. In the distance the
      carnal city, glistening next to the sea,
      and the
             emptiness
      of the desert, in a warm dry cocoon. I relaxed,
      took
      a deep
breath,
      and looked
      towards
         the moon.

                ::::::::::::::::::::

There he was, and he looked just like me. He had my face, my arms, legs, my eyes and lips, hair follicles falling exactly the same, that sweep of the brow, turn of the shoulder, stance, shift in the pelvis, pockets, a fondness for color, lapse, inclination to blinking. He stood on the opposite side of a line dividing me from me. He blinked. He shuffled. In an attempt to forgo similitude (impossible), I restrained myself.

I thought of taking a step forward. Dark purple arrows shot through the sky, sweeping in clouds, taking prisoners. Soldiers leered prismatic, inner skeletal structure of steel, blueprints, marks of construction, engravings of ownership. He did not own me. He looked like me but he wasn't me. He knew my secrets, from outside, cause and inter-action, a vilified shadow, but he wasn't.

Especial, a barrier grew between us, self and separation, my ghost. Surely he couldn't question this. And did I want him back, could I wonder, to think of absorbing. Metaphorically, though not in appearance, he had only one eye, and he kept secrets. His posture was not his own. The bastard had taken it upon himself to copy my shoes.

Could he, should he, would he know: the liar that is me, a lie. I'm not a fighter, and I'm not any good at keeping secrets. My games, my poetry, my language. No one listens to artist, not the artist himself; benumbing, I stuck, bleeding eye to eye to flaming banner, unable-no, not _willing_- to undertake filial significance. All my life I'd been too good at being _something_ like a person. To capture. What voracious weakness I. The keeping. No thought of (color). Not a glimpse of humanity.

To be an artifice one lie making voices and voice. I stumbled. Again. Stumble and choke. Lines of vivid color, distinguishing image and significance. A fondness for hearing myself speak: I like. Playing games- with:words. But; no(the liar) can never paint pictures enough. Shell of the shell, wanting for half a goddamn fucking name. Loss- time taking; no way(I've forgotten[how to speak]). Maybe in the past I'd fallen to the center of the universe. My disembodiment and my sense of the prophet. Death dying a whole unreal multitudinous ghost of voice.

::::::::::::::::::::

A great beast came roaring from the depths of the sea. Not to say I'm repeating myself, but the reptilian was clear in it, separating an element from the aqueous. Stepping heavily, on an indeterminate number of legs, it overturned ancient sand on the beach, into the canal, going against the water. It made its way to the bridge (jutting stone steal connecting land to land shit and flat surfaces cars emptiness and a big long row of yellow lines), and dropping, destroyed it: a shower of rock, falling into the water, crush and crash, this to destruction. Climbing outside, it sunk into buildings, destroying them; with some strange little panic for the virtual absence; no screaming, no blood streaming flesh in the bay. Underplaying destruction, it shore through a million dollars worth of glass, upturning cars, destroying the solidity of height, permanence and strength, petroleum syllables lining streets that ought to do a better job defending themselves. It roared. I realized it looked different from changing angles, growing heads, sprouting flaming tentacles, occasionally breathing a full flaring stream of fire, pure shining beams of plasma, bathing the world in acrid evening glows. Reaping death in the autumnal sun, a fanning swirl of leaves, debris and stuff all arching to some glutinous rainbow, it tore. Anthropomorphic claws. I thought of getting closer. Way back on the beach, watching it go, I though of clapping, as it put on quite the show.

Isn't it strange...

Sure

the hybrid crawling. It might be some ancient beast from a crevice way down in the sea, a genetic experiment or an alien baby taking inverted vengeance to defend the virginity of the sky. **Dust turned to flame**
and burned.

::::::::::::::::::::

up,
*Looking ^

I took   in
the sight   *

* of our
sacred *   *glow-* *holy mother,* *
ing gloriously
pale quiet reflecting *
* in the center of the sky*
a holy **moon**
blazing *

in stars, the perfection of
the night sky.
I would be going there soon, I would. From the top of a high
mountain: icy white beams shooting straight
metaphysical
presence the glory of release.

Down

below in the sickness of city, the world was nothing

but   plague, and I didn't have to complexion to make a home in

the valley

or starve all night in poor places, fearing sickness.
So transcendence absconded me,

freeing the body, up
to whatever grove of richness
on the surface of the moon.

I was going there,

I could.
Senseless as the gesture might be, I was sick
of climbing

high

mountains.

:::::::::::::::::::::

I met her atop a building. For miles a broken city spat plumes of fire, lighting vivid reflections of the sky, paths still gleaming in sea. We stood at an equal distance from each other, with the wind in our hair. I wanted to see her, couldn't stand to say goodbye: a problem. All my life I've never been good at letting go of things; not myself, not my trace in others. Drops of blood, from my arm and legs, beaded and fell. I stumbled.

"Do you really have to go?"

She nodded.

Do you really...

standing Munch shadows, solid color and a vague absence of shape. In her eyes reflecting the embers of this goddamn burning city: a sacrifice to whatever unnamed, unnoticed gods. Our capitalist fingers; never. Breath caught in my throat a pained tears of choking.

"Don't go," I said. "You can't."

She closed her eyes, long lashes touching together, fine fine darkness, held both arms to her chest. From here, intersecting, I could make out the mountains, the sea, the desert and the ruins of the city, smoldering now in gray folding tendrils to the tops and past every building, replacing clouds in the sky. If this were to be poetic, then fell a fine dusting of rain, but no rain came.

"I'll tell you my name," I said. "I promise."

She shook her head, lifting. Flashes and accumulation of jagged wavefront glorious center, she smiled (waving no no no no no) back choking savor monster glory tragic fading

:::::::::::::::::::::

He

took a step. I thought of walking but there was no fighting the nature of duality. Were we right, or really; it wasn't as though I were facing some fabulous new mystery, myself, the shadow of a shadow (no, my shadow's shadow); the smiling grinning mystery of me. He took another step forward, white teeth I never had to fight for, a smug sense of the accomplished.

But we couldn't talk we wouldn't, facing the impossibility of intersections. Horizontal between a glowing beam connected us, shining in the middle, thick pulsing as we moved. Could we tear, or would we, pushing past the obstacle that was we, accumulation of mind sight poetry, tearing old newspapers. Because of him I embraced the unreal, one eye, keeping secrets. Shadow creatures coming down-the walls: it

Could

we touch, or *were* we touching. Together what we were being. He defined me, escaped me, erasing me. Was that what? Undoing the ghost of a ghost. I never. The artist in me   No one listens to poets, for being impenetrable. Because I wasn't willing to try. They didn't give me free coffee anymore- they hadn't ever- and someday pimply headed kids the scum of alleyways might take my spot from me.

Approaching he was and smiled. Aphrodisiac my mind and bearing. He was me but he wasn't, I couldn't let. Our hands, palm and outstretched fingers. A wind picked up and flair;closer now we;stood and let- we never- closer fearing renewed separation denial still fucking LIAR LIAR LIAR the goddamn shitting pissing showering sun our outstretched hands palms crests and fingers we touched

we couldn't.

:::::::::::::::::::::

What do you want me to do?

he asked. There was nothing stranger than hearing the Chimera ask questions. In the distance still: spouting flame and danger. I didn't. I have no objections to losing my favorite spot. The spirit of the patriot is not strong in me.

"Probably leave it," I said. "It'll go away when it's had enough."

It cleaved, decapitating construction. Plaster showered blades of falling. Statues fell

monumentally, not screaming. They had more courage than I had, though similarly we suppressed the urge to care, not believing in some grander purpose, or the distinguished idea of a grander message. It upturned taxis, chewed through big signs, transformed. More shapes than one it shifted, a mass revolving. It wasn't very strong, but had the strength to lift at least one nuclear missile.

I clapped.

I told you you would need my help, he said.

"Have I told you thanks yet?"

I've heard you aren't very good with thanking.

"No," I said. "Not really.

::::::::::::::::::::

She rose.

I told her not to go, but she said she had to leave. All around us still the city burned, sifting in the graveyard, but no zombies came out, not feasting on car engines, burning holes by swallowing gallons of antifreeze. I held her for a moment, and kissed her, and she looked at me, beautifully, to say hello. It wasn't that I would miss her, though I would, but somewhere in me, where the demons aren't, she made me into something entirely different from myself, ghost mirror withheld image rewinding. She reminded me that I'd been to the center of the universe: that I'd journeyed deep into the forest, that I'd fallen into the water, that I'd gone to the moon. Glorious epicenter beacon of natural light, she was my vacant beautification and gorgeous moonlit dream, to prophecy, to dream. Spare pieces of her the stories held, nothing together but a tangled epigraph of contradicting voices, telling stories about hallways, about sitting. Everywhere I'd met her she'd never been alone, except for now, and when she was gone *I* would be alone. Sometimes I lied about her, I would lie: that I didn't see her face in others, that there wasn't such a thing. I know that really it's heartless of me, but I've never been one for sentimentality: all my life, if it is, if I haven't gone spiraling through some void in dimension, eating novas, drinking solar flares, prophesying to the cosmos and epic clouds of gaseous

Voices

dust... all my life, a journey toward, away from myself, as though I were more than (something) like a person, no artist the poet his fake fakery lie of a journey. I held her hand and made crazy declarations of love, some of them true, that might have made me cry, if I weren't crying already, to forsake unknowing, to cast aside some bountiful thing in myself. Behind us the sun the falling stars (finally finally falling) mountains sun sky desert the boundary of the sea a crying out a *flowing our* a rendezvous in heaven I really do I really the sacred rights a garden on the moon

    she
    left me

Voices

IV

(this is my
corner
)

Something quiet turned over in the darkness, a mouse (no not a sniffing mouse) in the way shadows have mixed with bands of diluted whiteness over sheet and fall and floorboard. Looking outside, I could make out part of the moon. It waved to me. I wondered if it were made of Brie. A cheesy moon: oddly distinguished. Calamity held hands in me and reaching out to (quiet) some tangled fold in me, hurting the hands to hold it.

For a while I thought of writing poetry, but grew frustrated with myself. All I ever think about is poetry; thus, there I have, I am and am not a poet. It doesn't leave any room for *me*, especially because my poetry can't belong to anyone else, it isn't poetry at all.

From

here

to

there

it flounces, baroque like Voltaire throwing (well meaning) hypocrisy at the very rich. I meant this to be peaceful, but I don't have what it takes for peace: coming back, maybe that's what's truly inhuman in me, I am.

::::::::::::::::::::

I thought for things to be right, I really did need to meet her here. My strangulated nightingale fantasy, altogether hopeless dream. I am. The strains of citizenship run through me, in who I am, what I do, the places I go, all I could ever hope *be*; drawing in reluctance from a whole whirlpool of stagnant resources, the world around me, the liberal artistic white male. I disgust myself.

As in all things, she is a part of me: separate. In all my life, I've encountered nothing not recollected; hearkening back to canonical readings of Plato. I am no stranger to trees, unsurprised by buildings, accustomed to bursts of unreality. I've been to the center of the universe many times, and I see in both directions. In(out)side myself, a prism of humanity. One eye. Two shadows.

If things were right I would meet her here, or she would be here already. Supine moonlight graciously flowing, the cool darkness of her lips hinting at mysterious varieties of expression; taking a step forward, back. I see in her many things; waxy stretches dark dark color, pale skin and secret body. If things were right, she would be here.

::::::::::::::::::::::

The disseminated soul drifts freely through space, swirling past planets and stars. The vacuum is strangely relaxing. The moon is actually made of old, old stones.

::::::::::::::::::::::

"Hello."
"Hello."
"I thought you would come."
"I have."
"It wouldn't be right," I said, "if you hadn't."
"Yeah," she said. "I know."

::::::::::::::::::::::

She tasted
like softness and moonlight: like purified water, more things than one. It isn't so hard to imagine, though really I find the less in touch I get with the world, the more   trouble
I have comprehending it: <u>analogous,</u> it is, this to that, I to her, this to being.
We were in a room.
It had doors and windows. Moonlight flooded from the windows. There was a bed. The walls were some gray plaster, I didn't care. There was a carpet. I wasn't alone. Contradicting forces layered polarity. I was here and I was really here. For the first time in so long, whatever, with a realization that I *am*, in relevance to time and place, the compound that is me, in tune. She was here with me, she was. This was the forth time I'd seen her, ripping holes in sensible arrangement. And I saw
the world from many angles: from all goddamn angles,
sides, up, front and back,

nineteen dimensions, physical, metaphysical,
    outside
        myself, inside, through the lens of
a camera, if that wasn't enough,
            realization
of separation.
        I had
        no shadow.
                        No.
                I had an *infinite*
                # of shadows, all around, defying the light, just like
her.
            At odds, we blocked
        out patterns in the light, coalescent to whatever form of togetherness.

                    ::::::::::::::::::::

"Do you really have to go?" I asked.
    She shook her head and I held her to me. Formless, shapeless, in being. I kissed her and told her maybe somewhere in me, if I was capable of love, that I felt it. The night unmasked itself to us, for the sense of poetry she invoked, or her certain things could be certain ways. Not the kind I care to understand. I held her and she reminded me of herself, of her figure in dreams. Our time together was nothing but a chronicle of breathing: body life and breath, delirious strivings. In her own way, she gave meaning to a whole history of silent voices, in me, in me: as though we had been here before,
    and someday soon,
    we would be here again.

*the page
that comes
after*